Critica

'This is a great holiday book!!! Think Tom Sharpe (Wilt, Riotous Assembly, etc) with balls. Royden manages to flesh out his "wacky characters" with just enough reality that even the cross-dressing Colonel and the unhinged, pot-smoking, Harley Davidson-riding Vicar of Buntleyford are believable (I think he was the Vicar at my last wedding actually). If you want a great laugh and you are not worried about the strange looks that you'll get on the plane when you pee yourself, then add it to your hand luggage!! Unfortunately I was on the No. 41 bus when I read it and am now being sued by The Hampshire Bus Cleaning Company!!! …I loved it!!...A gripping story that had me guessing to the end. If I could give it 6 stars, I would!'

Gary Shail - Quadrophenia

THE
DEALER

TONY ROYDEN

SHOTGUN PUBLISHING LTD

Special thanks to:
Jane Lester
Jana Tyrrell

Front cover graphics and knuckle-duster illustration
by Paul Baguley

Copyright © Tony Royden 2009

First published in Great Britain in 2009
by Shotgun Publishing Ltd.

www.thedealernovel.com

The right of Tony Royden to be identified as the author
of this work has been asserted by him in accordance
with the Copyright, Designs and Patents Act 1988.

ISBN: 978-0-9561253-0-9

Printed and bound in Great Britain by CPI Bookmarque, Croydon

Cover photograph copyright © Shotgun Publishing Ltd 2009

7:45 AM

Danny 'The Dealer' Dempsey slowly opened his eyes. His bedroom was dimly lit with rays of bright sunlight beaming through small gaps in the curtains. It was morning - that much Dealer could figure out as he lay motionless on his super-sized bed. On a cabinet close by sat the explanation for his current semiconscious state - a large bottle of whisky with three quarters missing, it also explained why he lay sprawled out on top of the bed sheets only half-undressed from the night before - seemed he just about managed to remove his trousers before collapsing.

Dealer coughed, his mouth dry and tasting vile. He slowly mustered up enough strength to roll over onto his side, then froze with horror. On the pillow next to his head sat a white envelope, his name:

'THE DEALER'

clearly hand-written on it. He was momentarily

stunned, his eyes opened wide, his mind racing to recall the previous night's events - then he freaked:

Grabbing a pistol from under his pillow, Dealer was up like a shot - nervous and breathing erratically. He circled the bedroom with the pistol held at arm's length - his heart pounding like a sledgehammer. There was an intruder, and considering The Dealer's notorious reputation, there could only be one policy in this situation - shoot first, torture the bastard for answers later.

He threw open the curtains, pistol swinging, his finger itching on the trigger ready to blow away anything that should move. The windows were all closed and intact, the locks were secure. He checked under the bed - nothing. He quickly rummaged through the wardrobes - again nothing. Dealer flung open the bedroom door, checking in all directions - the hallway was clear, but he was taking no chances. He cautiously edged his way out of the bedroom.

Questions were running through Dealer's head: If it was supposed to be a hit, then why didn't they finish him off while he slept? What better opportunity could there have been? He kicked open the bathroom door and swung the pistol inside, everything appeared to be how he had left it – although it took him a while to fathom as he left it in a complete mess – but the windows were secure, and that's all he really needed to know. More questions: A letter? Why break in to leave a letter? What's wrong with using the fucking letterbox?

Dealer was on edge – beads of sweat glistened on his forehead as he slowly made his way down a flight of stairs, his back pressed tightly against the wall. More questions: Why didn't the alarm go off? Was he so drunk that he foolishly forgot to set it?

He launched himself into the extended lounge, swinging the pistol in all directions - still nothing. The windows and outside doors were locked and secure.

Further questions: Could this letter be a warning? Was someone just trying to show how easy it would be to bump him off? But why issue a warning unless they wanted something in return? That's the way it worked with the underworld.

He made his way to a specially adapted utility room that catered for all his hi-tech security monitoring – the room was secure. A green light flashing on a keypad on the wall indicated that the alarm system had been activated. No, he had not been careless; the CCTV cameras outside were all showing on the monitors, everything was how it should be. He shook his head, perplexed. He wondered: Could the alarm be faulty? Or maybe the external siren had been tampered with? Was that why he hadn't heard the alarm going off? But that still didn't make sense, there were no signs of a forced entry - alarm or no alarm, an intruder would still need to break in.

Dealer was absolutely stumped, the whole house seemed to be secure, but his home had been violated and that scared the living shit out of him.

He made his way back upstairs and returned to the bedroom - the pistol still clutched firmly in his hand. He walked over to the bed, and stared long and hard at the envelope still resting on the pillow. He couldn't for the life of him figure out how it got there, but there were two further questions that needed answering: Who and why? He reflected on recent events…

In a quaint, picturesque English village surrounded by glorious countryside, rolling hills and trees in full bloom, Dealer could be seen out and about on an early morning stroll. It was a wonderfully warm summer morning, with endless blue skies and sunshine.

The former East London villain had opted for the quiet country life, not necessarily to escape from crime, but more an infatuation; Dealer had fallen in love with the stunning suburban village of Buntleyford on first sight, and moved there on a whim.

Although he was a notorious gangster, with a

reputation feared by many, Dealer also had charm and charisma, and was genuinely liked and respected by the village folk – who were, somewhat naively, unaware of his 'business activities'. He had settled in very quickly.

Black was Dealer's colour, and he was seldom seen wearing anything else. This warm August morning was no exception; Dealer was out ambling in his '20's style deluxe black pinstriped suit, black shirt, white spats and braces. He always looked the gangster – an image he was proud of.

70-year-old widow, Mrs Mildred Watts, opened her front door to take in the bottle of milk delivered daily to her doorstep. Mildred was always a ray of sunshine - upbeat, optimistic and full of smiles, she loved life and, since the death of her husband, really made an effort to live it to the full. Her true passion was cooking - in particular, baking, and her pies were legendary in the village. She bizarrely seemed to have a pie for every occasion, which wasn't always appropriate. Villagers still recall the time she turned up with a Banoffee Pie at the release of a much hated local paedophile, whilst the rest of Buntleyford turned up with pickets, petitions and a lot of hostility, eventually running the individual out of town and into hiding. But that was Mildred, she never heard further than 'village meeting...' before she got overexcited *and quickly drifted off into the land of luxury desserts.*

She spotted Dealer and quickly spruced herself up; she was never one to pass up the opportunity of a chat, especially with Dealer who she had taken a shine to.

Although she could only see the upper part of Dealer's body as he strolled on the other side of her garden wall, he appeared to be trailing a dog lead behind him. Mildred couldn't see the dog itself, but she never gave it a second thought. She quickly adjusted her hair ready to flirt:

'Morning, Danny!' she called.

'Mornin', Mrs Watts,' replied Dealer in a cheerful mood. 'You're lookin' lovely.'

Dealer always knew how to get Mildred going – flattery seemed to get him everywhere.

'Oh my,' she said bashfully, and readjusted her hair again. 'I feel a pie coming on,' she continued, flirtatiously raising her eyebrows several times.

Dealer smiled, he wasn't a big fan of pies, but he knew it kept Mildred happy so he gave her a friendly wink. Mildred was on top of the world - it was a great start to her day. She looked out to the glorious countryside surroundings:

'Fine morning, isn't it?' she said, exhilarated.

'Abso-fuckin'-brilliant,' answered Dealer.

Mildred let out a nervous laugh. 'Yes, indeed,' she

*agreed, not understanding Dealer's lingo. 'Abso...,
brilliant; as you say.'*

*Dealer gently tugged on the leash, and cheerfully
continued on his journey. Mildred watched admiringly
as he passed, and let out a heavy sigh –* Oh, if only he
was forty years older, *she thought.*

*A few houses further down, 75-year-old Christopher
Dingle, dressed in a tatty old dressing gown, was at
his front door picking up a newspaper left on his
doorstep. He spotted Dealer approaching, this time
the lower part of Dealer's body was obscured by
Christopher's privet hedge.*

'Good morning Danny!' shouted Christopher.

*'Alright, Chris,' replied Dealer in a friendly
manner. ''ow's the old tart?'*

*Christopher was momentarily baffled, then the
penny dropped:*

'OH! The wife. Yes, fine thank you.'

Dealer was suddenly pulled back by the dog lead:

*'Come on, you,' he said playfully, giving the lead a
gentle tug. Dealer was off moving again.*

*Christopher opened out the local newspaper and
read the front-page headline with concern: 'VILLAGE
CRIME UP 40%'. The decline of Buntleyford worried
Christopher immensely - he had lived in the village all
his life and had never felt more insecure. But he didn't
give himself much time to dwell on the issue, as his*

attention was quickly drawn to another disturbing headline: 'TWO DIE IN STONEBY'S ART RAID'. Christopher shook his head in despair as he turned back inside.

On the same stretch of road, a few houses further away, lived 68-year-old Betty Samuels. Betty was the self-appointed head of all the charity and fundraising activities for Buntleyford village, and she devoted all of her time to the various causes. Her organisational skills, coupled with her pushy nature, made her ideal for the position and she prided herself on always getting the job done. Aware of Dealer's growing popularity, Betty was very keen to involve him in her latest fundraising venture. As Dealer came into view over Betty's garden wall, she called out:

'Morning, Danny.'

'Mornin', Betty,' replied Dealer, hoping the conversation would end there.

'Didn't see you at the fete yesterday.'

'That's 'cos I wasn't fuckin' there,' said Dealer bluntly.

'Oh,' said Betty, taken aback. 'Well, that explains it.'

Dealer was pulled back by the lead:

'Not there, you filthy little shit!' he said with annoyance, then put the boot in – WHACK!

Betty could hear the muffled whimper of a

distressed animal coming from behind her wall; she struggled to see the beast.

'Sorry 'bout that,' said Dealer, shaking his head at something clearly untoward.

'That's okay,' replied Betty, unsure what the apology was actually for. But her mind was on more important matters:

'Danny, about the fundraising...'

'Yeah, yeah, no problem,' interrupted Dealer, 'we'll talk about it later,' he said unconvincingly, and was off walking again.

'Oh, okay,' said Betty, clearly defeated on this occasion, but knew there would be other opportunities - she was a determined woman.

As Dealer continued his stroll, he spotted ex-army war hero Jack Houseman, locally known as 'The Colonel'. He was meticulously trimming his privet hedge with a rusty pair of garden shears, whilst proudly wearing his army jacket and displaying his war medals. The 79-year-old Colonel had become a tad senile in his ageing years, but he still hadn't lost his flamboyant personality nor his forthright manner.

As Dealer approached, the Colonel stopped trimming, and, in true military style, rose to attention and saluted:

'Morning Dempsey!' said the Colonel, in an authoritative and braying voice.

'Mornin' Colonel,' replied Dealer, without breaking stride. 'At ease, old son.'

'Oh, I see you have an animal,' remarked the Colonel disapprovingly. 'A filthy, rotten, stinking animal! Is it a bitch?'

'Yeah, a right fucker,' confirmed Dealer.

'Thought so. Still, at least you have it muzzled.'

'Wouldn't 'ave it any other way.'

'Good man, Dempsey. Carry on!'

The Colonel watched Dealer amble away, then muttered to himself:

'Damn flea-ridden blighters - menace to society!'

At that moment a bluebottle landed on the Colonel's backside and he went to swat it with his hand - SLAP! - 'Oh', thought the Colonel with surprise as his hand hit the bare skin of his behind. It was only then he realised that he had forgotten to get properly dressed that morning. As he stood in his front garden behind the privet hedge, the Colonel was completely naked from the waist down, his bare bottom unashamedly visible for all of his next-door neighbours to see.

Dealer continued his casual stroll, and soon reached the vicarage. The front door opened and the vicar, The Reverend Oliver Moore, or 'The Minister' - as he was more commonly known - emerged clutching a crash helmet.

The Minister, a longstanding member of the clergy at Buntleyford village, was loved and respected by all; his caring and charitable nature, together with his good humour and charm, had made him a village favourite.

But in his advancing years - now 60 and counting - traces of a rather different persona had begun to emerge; the Minister had become very sarcastic - with an extremely dry sense of humour that some would say verged on the outright insulting. His once caring nature also seemed to have waned somewhat – as though he were fed up of always being the 'Good Samaritan' when there seemed to be very little reward. This noticeable change was not helped by the rising crime-rate the village was suffering – his endless efforts were slowly wearing him down.

The Minister spotted Dealer passing. The lower part of Dealer's body once again hidden, this time by the vicarage's wooden fence boundary. The Minister noticed that Dealer trailed a dog leash and appeared to be out walking a pet – not a familiar sight for the Minister, but he thought nothing of it and called out:

'Morning, Danny!'

'Mornin', Vicar.'

'Uhmm.. Have you given any thought to our little..er… local problem, we spoke about?' he asked hesitantly.

'Don't worry, Padre,' replied Dealer, 'I'm takin' care of it, even as we speak.'

The Minister wasn't convinced, and traits of his new-found sarcasm surfaced:

'Yes...of course you are,' he said with a deadpan expression.

The Minister couldn't be bothered to pursue the conversation. 'Well, bless you, Danny.'

'And you, Vicar,' replied Danny, clumsily airing the sign of the cross, whilst muttering to himself, 'and all that bollocks.'

Dealer was again pulled back by the dog lead. He was beginning to get agitated with his disobedient pet.

The Minister put on his crash helmet and headed down an alley to the side of the vicarage. He climbed onto a enormous vintage Harley Davidson motorbike - customised with monstrous wheels and extended handlebars - reminiscent of the bike ridden by actor Peter Fonda in the film 'Easy Rider' – which happened to be one of the Minister's favourite movies. He kick-started it, then revved it up - again and again, continuously, for no reason other than that he loved the sound of the roaring engine.

Across the road from the vicarage, in a small cottage, 63-year-old Fanny Tattle was once again startled awake by the Minister's Harley. She crawled out of bed, extremely fed up, and made her way over to the window, just in time to see the Minister wheel-spinning around in circles.

'For goodness' sake,' she muttered to herself.

Fanny was convinced the Minister was going through a late mid-life crisis – as this was not the normal behaviour one would expect from a 60-year-old vicar in a small English village.

After several manic circles, with the Minister screaming at the top of his voice like a crazed cowboy riding in a wild-west rodeo, the bike screeched away to a thunderous sound, leaving a mass-cloud of polluted smoke and fumes.

Fanny was unimpressed and extremely peeved. She clearly remembered the basic rules of house buying, and recited to herself the advice she had been given at the time:

'Don't buy near a school, don't buy near a bus stop, or a fire station, or a pub! That's what they told me,' she recalled. 'Didn't mention anything about a friggin' vicarage! Did they – Noooooo.'

As the smoke began to clear, Fanny recognised the figure of Dealer:

'Hmm, didn't know Danny had a dog,' she mumbled to herself.

As more of the smoke settled, Fanny became even more puzzled:

'What on earth...?' she said, struggling to work out

what sort of dog it was. It was the most peculiar shape
- not at all dog-like.

After a short while when the smoke had finally
cleared, Fanny had to rub her eyes several times over:

'Oh...my...God,' she said in disbelief.

Dealer forcefully tugged on the leash:

'Will you come on!' he demanded.

Attached to the end of the dog lead was 21-year-
old local tearaway Jimmy Todd sporting a dog collar
around his neck. Jimmy was on his knees with his feet
bound together, hands tied behind his back and duct
tape over his mouth. He looked battered, bloodied and
exhausted. There was genuine fear in his eyes; Jimmy
was well aware of Dealer's reputation and how he
had earned his nickname - it had nothing to do with
drugs or playing cards:

In Danny 'The Dealer's' younger days working
under the wing of ageing East London Don, Joey
Nelson, Danny was the entrusted gang member that
Joey would send in - normally as a last resort - to sort
out any problems the 'firm' had:

'Leave it with me, I'll deal with it,' Danny would
calmly say, and 'deal' with it he did – occasionally
with diplomacy, sometimes with intimidation, but
mostly with brutal and senseless violence. Whatever
the method, Danny always dealt with it, and rapidly

gained a reputation accordingly.

For Joey Nelson, 'Send in The Dealer' became a favourite phrase of his – a nickname that stuck.

WHACK! - *Dealer booted Jimmy again, who let out another muffled whimper.*

Fanny watched from the window, her mouth agape, flinching as the boot connected:

'Oh I get it,' she said sarcastically, 'it must be 'kick-a-yob' week.'

Dealer coolly continued his stroll with Jimmy inching along on his knees.

'Easier to train a fuckin' chimp,' muttered Dealer under his breath.

Dealer was focused on the envelope that lay on his bed. Still apprehensive and confused he approached with caution. Holding the gun at arm's length, he used the barrel to carefully flip the envelope over, then let out a small sigh of relief - the envelope was very light and unsealed, it couldn't be a bomb.

Gaining courage, Dealer gently picked up the envelope and held it up to the light. He examined it closely and could see nothing unusual, so he removed the two-page 'letter' from within.

He sat himself down on the bed, discarded the envelope, and began to read. Furrows appeared on his forehead, he was clearly puzzled, and the more he read the more apprehensive he became. Very soon the 'letter' was beginning to scare him. He finished reading the first page and was up on his feet pacing the room anxiously as he read the second. His breathing became heavy, his hands trembling - the second page was even more disturbing. By the time he had finished reading he was dumbfounded.

He slowly lowered the 'letter', deep in thought, then rushed to a cabinet. He threw open a drawer and frantically rummaged through it until he found a sheet of paper - another letter - which he scrutinised. He held it up alongside the original 'letter' and examined them both together, his eyes scanning from one to the other - comparing the two. A sudden sense of urgency overcame Dealer, he hastily grabbed his mobile phone - along with his trousers - and exited in a hurry.

8:02AM

In a bedroom in the West-End of London, gangster Donald Kelly lay awake on his four-poster bed, deeply troubled.

His bedroom was lush and very traditional throughout; classic paintings adorned the walls - all hanging in their original ornate gilt frames, an elaborate ten bulb crystal chandelier hung from the ceiling, and Georgian furniture was gracefully placed in all four corners of the room.

39-year-old Donald was a ruthless villain, who just happened to have a taste for the finer things in life. His knowledge of art and antiques was second to none, and he prided himself on having a small fortune in collectibles – of which very few were obtained legitimately:

Donald began his 'working' life as a bare-knuckle street-fighter and, having brutally disposed of anyone who dared challenge him, had decided to handle his own 'purse'; clobbering anyone who dare try to muscle in, or attempt to short change him. He had an enormous build, with fists twice the size of the average man. The natural contours of his face lent him a fierce and menacing look, and he soon realised that he could put the fear of God into people with just one snarl. Donald quickly rose in the ranks of the underworld and built an empire upon intimidation and extortion.

Seldom did Donald show emotion, he was normally a calm and calculating individual, but on this particular day he was unsettled.

He climbed out of bed and slipped on a blue silk robe, then made his way to where a small antique cabinet sat in the corner of the room. Pushing aside the cabinet, he revealed a combination safe embedded in the wall, and quickly entered the six-digit combination number. The safe's door swung open - Donald reached inside and produced two rolled up Picasso paintings…

It was the annual fundraising summer fete for Buntleyford village, held at the local boatyard. It was a hot afternoon and the event was in full swing, the village locals were out enjoying the entertainment.

Children were gathered around a blow-up

paddling pool, all holding toy rods, trying to fish themselves a plastic duck containing a winning prize number.

Mildred Watts was in her element, busy selling her home-made cakes - always a great money-spinner for fundraising, this particular year being no exception, with the cake queue stretching beyond her stall and around the corner.

Betty Samuels, the fete organiser, was running the tombola stand, with an array of donated prizes lined up on a table behind her. Christopher Dingle had just purchased a winning ticket and was eagerly awaiting his prize.

'There we go, Chris. Number two-seven-one,' said Betty with a smile, handing him the prize his wife had donated only the previous day. It was a bright green and red flowered ceramic vase; a Christmas present that Christopher had bought for his wife, that she had never liked and was happy to see the back of. Although offended, Christopher, for a quiet life, chose not to say anything about her donation, and was now pleasantly surprised to see the vase again:

'Oh,' he smirked, 'the old tart will be delighted,' he said to Betty with a wink.

At the coconut shy, the Minister launched a wooden ball – it flew through the air and rocked a coconut, but it failed to tumble. The waiting crowd *surrounding him all sighed loudly with one voice, and the Minister pretended to be playfully vexed. He began swinging his arm around in 360-degree circles – winding up his last ball, and, à la James Brown in his deep-south gospel preacher role in 'The Blues Brothers' (another favourite movie of his), yelled out:*

'Oooooooo, you're going down, you hairy mother......superior!'

He launched the ball...SMACK! It was a direct hit - the coconut fell and the crowd cheered. The Minister clenched his fist in jubilation as the stall's proprietor handed him a coconut.

As the Minister turned to walk away, he was startled to find himself confronted by a nun:

'Oh,' said the Minister somewhat embarrassed, and hoping she hadn't heard the 'hairy mother superior' slur – especially as the head of the convent was somewhat moustachioed.

The nun smiled knowingly – she had heard it alright.

'Err... Not you, Mother... Superior... er... Sister,' fumbled the Minister. 'Here, have a coconut,' he said, thinking fast, and handed her his prize.

The nun's face lit up, she was delighted – she welcomed the offering and couldn't wait to show it off at the convent. The Minister wiped his brow with relief as he turned away, muttering under his breath:

'Yeah, give my regards to Old Mother Goatee.'

Over at the buzzer game, with an intense look of concentration, was seven-year-old Emma. She slowly manoeuvred a hooped metal ring carefully around a twisting and winding metal wire frame, and was doing exceptionally well. The crowd that had gathered watched with bated breath as Emma neared the end of the puzzle, when suddenly – BUZZZZZZZZZ! she flinched as the hoop touched the wire frame.

The electrical wires attached to the buzzer ran all the way to a nearby boathouse where Tommy Parker - a small-time gangster – was gagged and strapped to a chair, with the wires running up his trouser leg and attaching to his genitals.

Unbeknown to Emma, and the rest of the village folk, the buzzer game had been sabotaged and specially adapted by Donald Kelly's gang the night before. Simultaneously as the buzzer sounded, Tommy violently jerked in the chair - his muscles contorting with every electric shock.

Standing behind Tommy, looking extremely intimidating, were two of Donald's henchmen affectionately known as 'The Twins' - identical in every way; both 6ft 4" tall, dressed in black suits and wearing dark glasses. The Twins tended to do everything telepathically and in unison – almost robot-like. It was uncanny the way they just seemed to

21

instinctively know when the other was going to do anything – walk, reach, crouch, drink or even talk, and the other would just follow suit. They stood, cold-faced and unapproachable, legs astride with their hands clasped behind their backs. Then, as one, they brought their legs together and arms around, folding them at the front. It was done with such precision, that for an outsider it may have looked rehearsed, but it wasn't - there was just an unfathomable cohesion between the two.

Donald Kelly stood at the window watching Emma at the buzzer game. He smiled:

'Oh dear, not very good, is she?' he remarked sarcastically.

The buzzer noise stopped, and Tommy's body slumped in the chair, his head dropping to his chest as he struggled to get his breath back.

Standing next to Tommy was Donald's trusty, but not too bright, henchman - Mickey McColl - who was loving every second. It was his device that Tommy was strapped to, and it was working a charm. Mickey was wearing a psychotic smile and nodded his head with delight as he looked over to Donald for praise of his work. But Donald was unmoved, he snapped his fingers and pointed to Tommy's head. Mickey quickly wiped the smirk off his face and acknowledged - pulling the gag away from Tommy's mouth. Tommy was disoriented and tearful. He winced like a baby.

'Can you remember anything yet, Tommy?' asked Donald calmly.

Tommy wept uncontrollably and was in considerable pain, he tried to speak but his words were distorted into a mass of high-pitched unintelligible gobbledegook – sounding almost bird-like. He was clearly traumatised.

Donald was aware of the general consensus that a good squeeze of the testicles could add a few octaves to the vocal chords, and this certainly seemed to be the case with Tommy. Donald screwed up his face as he tried to pick out the words. Mickey also screwed up his face – aping Donald. Donald and Mickey turned to each other and shrugged their shoulders – between them they couldn't understand a single thing Tommy was trying to say.

Donald snapped his fingers and pointed to Tommy's head. Mickey quickly responded and replaced the gag. Donald beckoned Mickey over to him.

'Yes boss?' wondered Mickey, in his normal gormless fashion.

'Mickey, when you said you were gonna make him sing like a canary...?' enquired Donald, hoping for an intelligent answer.

Mickey was completely lost. 'Yes boss?' he replied

blankly.

Donald waited a second, hoping Mickey's vacant expression would change – but it didn't:

'Never mind,' said Donald, exasperated.

He walked back over to Tommy:

'Look Tommy, I'm a reasonable man,' explained Donald patronisingly. 'Give me the paintings and I'll let you live. I can't be fairer than that.'

Tommy was petrified. He looked at Donald with uncertainty, then over his shoulder to the giant Twins, who simultaneously stepped forwards and dropped their hands to the side, clenching their fists and cracking their knuckles. Tommy didn't like the options presented to him, but he had no choice – he nodded reluctantly.

'Good boy. Now where are they?' asked Donald sternly.

With his wrists strapped to the chair, Tommy pointed a finger and beckoned Donald over to where an umbrella lent up against a wall. Donald strolled towards it, looking back at Tommy's pointed finger to double-check if he was heading in the right direction. He curiously picked up the brolly:

'What?... This?'

Tommy nodded.

'You better not be fuckin' with me!' threatened Donald.

The Twins surged forward, each putting a firm hand on Tommy's shoulders. Tommy flinched and then panicked, shaking his head frantically to reassure Donald that he wasn't messing. Donald closely examined the brolly, turning it every which way. He held it upside down and noticed a 5-inch metal tip. Glancing over to Tommy, he pointed to the tip - Tommy nodded. Donald carefully unscrewed the metal tip and gave the brolly a gentle shake - out popped two rolled up paintings.

Donald was apprehensive but excited, he quickly discarded the brolly and unrolled the paintings. His face lit up as he looked at them in awe:

'Oh yes,... oh fuckin' yes.'

As one, The Twins released their grip from Tommy's shoulders and took a step backwards, placing their arms back into the folded position. Tommy let out a huge sigh of relief and sank into the chair.

Mickey walked over to Donald. He too looked at the paintings admiringly:

'Are they genuine Cappuccino's, boss?' he asked, intrigued.

Donald rolled his eyes at Mickey's ignorance. Suddenly a succession of buzzes could be heard – BUZZ! BUZZ! BUZZ! BUZZ! - Tommy jerked violently in the chair. The buzzing continued.

'What the fuck?...' wondered Donald.

Donald and Mickey peered out from the boathouse window to where a three-year-old girl played the buzzer game. She thought the buzzer noise was hilarious, and laughed out loud as she continually hit the metal hoop against the wire frame – BUZZ! BUZZ! BUZZ!!!

Donald was still crouched by the safe in his bedroom holding the rolled up paintings, he was deeply concerned. He stood up and carried the paintings over to a black executive briefcase resting on an antique chest of drawers. Opening the case, he placed the paintings inside – it was decision time. Uncharacteristically, he seemed unsure of himself, a big part of him just wanted to put the paintings back inside the safe. He took a few seconds to weigh up his options - something he had been doing constantly for the past 24-hours, then reluctantly made a decision – and slammed the case shut.

8:10AM

35-year-old Alan Worrell, or 'Bolt' as he was better known to his friends, lay asleep in his bed. His bedside phone began to ring, and Bolt sprung up - startled and disorientated. He quickly regained his composure and reached for the handset:

"ello Dealer.......yeah I'm awake,' he said rubbing his eyes. 'Umm... yeah I know it .....okay, I'll be there....see ya.'

He replaced the receiver and yawned - still half asleep.

Bolt was a giant heavyweight of a man, built of solid muscle, but he rarely needed to use force - his sheer physical presence was enough to frighten the crap out of most people.

He was rubbing the stubble on his chin, still in a dozy state, when he spotted his crossbow resting on a chair…

Bolt and close friend Charlie 'The Bat' Hemmings were in the village of Buntleyford walking rapidly towards the giant gates of Dealer's fortress home. Bat wore thick lens glasses and had obvious trouble seeing - this was evident from the way he walked. He was constantly veering off course, with Bolt repeatedly grabbing him by the shoulder and dragging him back – reminding Bolt of his childhood and walking his over-excited puppy on a lead. Bat was short and podgy, and not the brightest of people, but he was one of the family (so to speak), having grown up with both Bolt and Dealer in East London.

They arrived at the gate and Bolt pressed an intercom button. He glanced across to where he thought Bat was standing, only to see that Bat hadn't stopped and was still walking rapidly away.

'BAT!' he shouted with annoyance.

Bat instantly about-turned and hastily headed back - thinking that Bolt had discovered something of interest en route:

'You found some dosh?' asked Bat, eyes gleaming with excitement, eagerly searching the ground.

'Fuck's sake,' said Bolt, 'we're 'ere!'

Dealer was inside, sitting smugly in a big comfy leather armchair and puffing on a giant cigar, when he heard the buzzer and was instantly up. He checked a security monitor by the front door - it was his pals, so he pressed a button to unlock the gate. Dealer left the front door ajar, returned to his chair and waited.

'Come on,' said Bolt, grabbing Bat by the shoulder and leading him in.

Moments later they had entered Dealer's home, and Bolt steered Bat into the front room. As they entered, Bat was looking in all directions:

'Alright Dealer?' he asked excitedly, unsure where to direct his greeting.

'Alright Bat,' replied Dealer.

Bat pinpointed Dealer's position and stuck his thumbs up with satisfaction.

'Sorry we're late, Dealer,' said Bolt.

'That's alright, Bolt, my guest 'ere has been keepin' me entertained,' said Dealer.

Bolt was puzzled. 'Who the fuck is that?' he asked.

In a corner of the room was Jimmy Todd on his knees, still bound and gagged and looking petrified.

''That',' explained Dealer, 'is my guest.'

Bat circled the room in confusion looking for the visitor.

Dealer turned to Jimmy and picked up the leash still attached to his neck:

'Well, say 'ello then!'

Dealer yanked hard on the lead, and Jimmy let out a muffled squeal. Bat's face suddenly lit up. He crouched down in excitement:

'Oh excellent. What's its name?'

Dealer was bemused by the question:

'Jimmy Todd,' replied Dealer, wearily.

'Brilliant!' said Bat, and began slapping his knees.
'Here Jimmy, come on boy, come on.'

Bolt buried his head in his hands.

'For fuck's sake, Bat!' said Dealer.

'What?' asked Bat innocently.

*'When are you gonna get yer fuckin' eyes sorted
out?!' Dealer continued.*

'Why?.... Is he sleepin'?' wondered Bat.

*'No,' explained Dealer sarcastically, 'he's 'avin' a
dump!'*

*'Oh, sorry, Dealer.... Sorry Jimmy.' apologised
Bat with embarrassment.*

Bolt quickly changed the subject:

'So what's on yer mind, Dealer?'

*'I've been asked to help out with a little local
problem, Bolt; wonder if you boys can lend a hand?
Should be a few bob in it for ya.'*

*'No problem, Dan,' said Bat supportively. 'I got
nothin' better to do today.'*

'Yeah, why not,' agreed Bolt.

*'Thanks, I appreciate it,' said Dealer, then stood to
face Jimmy. 'First, we need to extract a few names
from our little friend 'ere.'*

Dealer's expression quickly turned to an evil smile.

Bolt stood alongside Dealer, also wearing the same evil grin. Jimmy was terrified, tears rolled down his cheeks. Bat then stood alongside Bolt - totally baffled:

'You mean, it talks?!'

Fifteen minutes later, Dealer, Bolt and Bat were standing in the street outside the gates of Dealer's home. In Dealer's hand was a piece of paper containing a list, which he carefully tore into three pieces:

'Right, boys,' said Dealer, as he began to distribute the pieces, 'that's for you, Bolt.'

'Got it,' said Bolt, examining his portion of the list.

'Bat, you take care of this,' continued Dealer.

'Right,' said Bat, clutching the list with zeal.

'And I'll sort this lot out,' finished Dealer. 'Let's meet back 'ere when we're all done.'

'Right,' agreed Bolt.

'Got ya,' confirmed Bat, and they all headed off in different directions.

No sooner had they dispersed, when Fanny Tattle appeared. She meandered toward Dealer's home and stopped:

'Oh...my...God,' she said to herself in shock.

Fanny could see Jimmy Todd, still bound and gagged, dangling upside down by his feet out of a second floor window of Dealer's home. Fanny stared in disbelief:

'Oh yeah,' she sarcastically recalled, 'don't buy a house near a lunatic.'

Later that day, Bolt was coolly resting up against the door of his parked car – a jet-black, top of the range 7 series BMW, in a large car park. As he patiently waited, his ears pricked up when he heard the distant sound of a speeding car coming towards him. The noise became very loud very quickly, and within seconds a stolen car, driven by two teenage joy riders, suddenly skidded into the car park and raced straight past him. Bolt didn't flinch.

The driver of the vehicle expertly manoeuvred a 180-degree handbrake turn - wheel-spinning with smoke exuding from the rear tyres as it burnt rubber, then screeched off at high speed.

Bolt was unimpressed. He calmly opened the boot of his BMW, reached in, and produced a crossbow. Bolt's reputation in the underworld had evolved from his strange and obsessive fascination with the crossbow - which also lent to his nickname, and although he knew it was not the most efficient of modern day weaponry – difficult to conceal and horrendously longwinded to reload, he loved the way it felt in his hands, how cool he looked with it, and the way it made him stand out from other gangsters. He also adored the fact that they were not illegal to own.

Whilst the boy-racer skilfully weaved his way in and out of parked cars at high speed, Bolt calmly and effortlessly pulled back the string and cocked the crossbow. He slid a shining silver bolt into position, then held it up to his eye and adjusted the sight.

Once again the car shot past Bolt - the boys screaming at the top of their voices as the adrenaline rush took over. Bolt coolly took aim, and, as the driver attempted another 180-degree handbrake turn, Bolt squeezed the trigger and fired – BANG!! - A rear tyre exploded, sending the car spinning out of control and smashing into a parked vehicle.

Bolt smugly swung the crossbow across his shoulder, and stood proudly admiring his handiwork - it gave him an immense feeling of power. After a few moments of wallowing in self-congratulation, he placed the crossbow back into the boot, and casually made his way over to the smouldering wreck. He threw open the driver-side door, leant in and smiled:

"ello boys. 'ow the fuck are ya?'

The teenage boys: 18-year-old driver, Sean and his 17-year-old passenger, Frederick, were shell-shocked and battered. Sean was slumped over the steering wheel holding his ribcage in agony, a gaping wound on his forehead; Frederick was holding what was clearly a broken nose, blood was running down his

33

chin and onto his white T-shirt. They were both dazed,
but completely taken aback by the monstrous figure of
Bolt bearing down on them.

Bolt began to tut:

'Oh dear,' he said patronisingly, 'no seat belts.'

He reached in and grabbed the pair by the scruffs
of their necks:

'Silly boys,' said Bolt, as he dragged them from the
vehicle.

Bolt was focused on the crossbow - still smiling to
himself. A quick glance at the clock suddenly kicked
him into gear. He climbed out of bed and stretched
out, then fell to the floor to begin his morning ritual of
press-ups.

8:13 AM

The curtains were drawn, and Jerry Coe was snuggled up in bed with his wife, Maureen, who was five months pregnant. The bedroom was very plain, the furniture old and worn, and it was evident that 40-year-old Jerry was not one of the more successful gangsters. In fact, most wouldn't consider him to be a gangster at all; Jerry was just a simple bookkeeper who had naively got involved with the wrong people, and soon reached a point where he couldn't turn back. He was a happy-go-lucky individual who never liked making waves, easy to get on with, and was genuinely liked and trusted within the London gangster circle. Sadly though, his easy-going nature meant he was often taken advantage of - he was indeed a pauper amongst kings.

Jerry slithered down the bed sheets and placed his ear on Maureen's protruding stomach.

'Well?' asked Maureen.

'Yeah...' replied Jerry in amazement, 'I can actually hear the sea!'

Maureen ruffled his hair in a friendly manner:

'You nutter.'

Jerry snuggled up again. They were a very happy couple.

'It's amazing. I can't wait to be a dad,' said Jerry excitedly. 'Guess what, Maur?'

'What?'

'I could have a nice little bonus coming my way today.'

'Really, Jerry?' asked Maureen tentatively. 'Enough for a decent car or holiday?'

'Maybe more,' replied Jerry, and smiled suggestively…

In a lush high-rise office, overlooking Piccadilly Circus in London's West-End, Jerry sat himself down across a huge antique mahogany desk, opposite Donald Kelly. Donald's office was not dissimilar to his home; the walls were adorned with classic paintings, a sparkling cut crystal chandelier hung from the ceiling, the furniture was antique, there was a luxuriant deep red carpet, and the centre piece - Donald's pride and joy - a 17th century fireplace mantle, inlaid with intricate hand carved sculptures.

Either side of a giant oak office door were Donald's henchmen The Twins – themselves standing like carved sculptures, motionless and menacing - still wearing dark glasses, both with legs slightly astride and hands interlocked to the front of them. Between them was Mickey, frantically chewing on a piece of gum, slouched with his back against the door awaiting instructions. He blew a small bubble that burst around his top lip – which he easily managed to scoop off with his tongue, and was back frantically chewing again.

Jerry opened up a large ledger book.

'So what 'ave we got?' enquired Donald.

'Not too much this week, Don,' replied Jerry, referring to the ledger. 'Ray Vallone - payment three days late.....The Gartshore brothers - one week overdue.....and that twat Bates still hasn't come good.'

'Oh fuckin' dear,' grunted Donald. 'Okay boys,' he said turning to his heavies. 'Go do your....'

Donald was somewhat surprised to see that Mickey had blown another bubble, which had got so big it was hiding most of his face – then it burst - POP! - leaving pink gum stuck to his eyebrows.

'....stuff,' continued Donald in disbelief.

'Right, boss,' said Mickey unfazed, and enthusiastically opened the door to leave.

Jerry had to force himself not to laugh, and put a

hand over his mouth to hide his amusement.

Donald suddenly remembered. 'Oh Mickey,' he called.

'Yes, boss?' said Mickey turning back, and picking at a bit of gum stuck to the end of his nose.

'Try to get the money first; don't break their fingers and then lead them to a fuckin' cash machine ...like last week,' pleaded Donald.

'Oh, right,' said Mickey, who hadn't a clue what Donald was talking about. 'Got it, boss.'

As Mickey headed out, The Twins turned in unison and followed Mickey for their 'debt collecting' duties, leaving Donald shaking his head in despair:

'Loyal as fuck, but not too much in the Stephen Hawking's department,' he explained to Jerry whilst tapping his own head to illustrate his point.

Jerry smiled openly, he knew exactly what Donald meant, but always found Mickey to be great entertainment.

'I've got a bit of a problem, Jerry,' continued Donald, looking troubled.

'What's up, Don?'

Donald stood to admire some of the paintings on the wall:

'I've got myself a couple of Picasso's.'

Jerry was shocked:

'Not the ones from Stoneby's auction house?'

'The very same.'

'Fuck. Donald, you're asking for serious trouble there,' said Jerry with genuine concern.

'Don't I know it - some of the best art ever produced and I can't even hang 'em up to enjoy.'

'My advice, Donald, is burn them and scatter the ashes.'

'You know I can't do that, Jerry,' said Donald calmly.

Jerry sympathised with Donald's love of art:

'No, I guess not. Look, Don, why don't I have a word with Scott Flowers.'

'Flowers!!' snapped Donald disapprovingly.

'I know you don't like him...'

'I fuckin' hate that little prick!!'

'But we only need him for his contacts - just as a go-between. If there's anyone out there willing to deal in some extremely hot paintings, Scott can find them.'

Donald wasn't convinced:

'I dunno, Jerry. Somethin' about him makes my skin crawl.'

'I know,... but I can't think of anyone better; Scott will get you top dollar.'

Donald pondered, he knew his options were limited. Jerry sat silently watching as Donald paced the office mulling over his suggestion with mixed emotions.

A few days later, Jerry was waiting outside a busy Premiership football ground surrounded by a mass of supporters flooding through the turnstiles. It was FA cup quarterfinal day, and a capacity crowd was expected.

Jerry was anxiously looking in all directions when he was tapped on the shoulder. He spun around to face his old friend - North London villain, Scott Flowers. They were excited to see each other and instantly embraced.

'Scotty! Good to see you,' said Jerry with a huge smile.

'And you, Jez. How's Maureen?' asked Scott.

'Yeah she's fine - five months pregnant,' replied Jerry proudly.

'Fuckin' brilliant, congratulations.'

'Cheers mate.'

Jerry produced two tickets for the match and waved them at Scott:

'Shall we?'

'Lead the way!' said Scott enthusiastically.

A short while later, Jerry and Scott were inside the ground, seated amongst a sea of red with all the Liverpool supporters who had travelled to see the game. Scott was an avid Liverpool fan, but rarely got to see his beloved team play, so this was a rare treat for him, and he was buzzing. Liverpool were playing Chelsea, a formidable opponent, the match was in progress, it was tense, both teams had missed a number of chances and the atmosphere was electric.

Jerry had one eye on the game – he too loved football and supported the reds, but he needed to talk business:

'...so it's important they go to a good home - you know what Donald's like with his art,' explained Jerry.

'So what's in it for me, Jez?'

'Ten percent of whatever you can get.'

Scott smiled approvingly:

'Excellent, leave it with me.'

Suddenly there was an air of excitement - a Liverpool striker was heading for goal, when out of nowhere a Chelsea defender slid in and took the legs from under him. The crowd were up on their feet in unison, booing and jeering. Scott was irate:

'FUCK'S SAKE REF. SEND HIM OFF!! Dirty bastard!'

As Scott slowly sat back down with the rest of the fans, he continued talking business as though nothing had happened:

'Actually,' said Scott calmly, keeping his eyes on the game, 'I was wondering if I can interest you in something, Jez.'

'Go on,' said Jerry, intrigued.

'A very quick earner - buy from man A, sell to man B - 50 gees profit for an hour's work.'

'That simple?'

'Oh yeah, I've done it twice already - safe as houses. Trouble is, this time I haven't got the cash to do the deal with man A.'

'How much' you need?'

'100 gees.'

Jerry was shocked:

'Phew, sorry Scott, I haven't got that sort of money.'

'Yeah, but Donald has.'

Jerry laughed:

'Yeah right, are you gonna ask him?'

'Hear me out, Jez. You control Donald's lending empire, right?'

'Well, yeah...'

'So you advance me the cash without writing it in the ledger, and I'll get it back to you within 24 hours - before Donald even knows it's missing - plus 25 gees for yourself.'

Jerry was still unsure:

'You make it sound so easy.'

'It is easy, Jez, trust me.'

Jerry dwelt on the proposition for a moment. He had never done anything like this before, but Scott *was a mate, and it was tempting. Scott continued:*

'It will be the quickest earner you've ever had.'

'But if it's late, I'll have to log it - I'll have to tell Donald, and God fuckin' help you.'

'Don't worry, Jez - safe as houses.'

Their conversation was interrupted by the match - a fantastic flying header completely out of the blue by a Liverpool midfielder, the ball rocketed into the roof of the Chelsea net. The crowd erupted. Both Jerry and Scott were up on their feet celebrating:

'YEAHHHHHHHHH!!!!!!!!'

'Fuckin' brilliant!' said Scott, jubilantly.

Jerry's celebration was short-lived, as he was still mulling over the offer. He thought of all the things he could do with 25 grand to make a better life for his wife and forthcoming kid:

'Okay, I'll have the cash for you tomorrow morning,' shouted Jerry over the roaring crowd.

Scott smiled:

'COME ON YOU REDS!!'

Jerry snuggled up to his wife in bed.

'Oh Jerry, wouldn't it be wonderful to have a holiday?' said Maureen longingly.

Jerry was beaming, he felt that it could be his day:

'It's looking good, Maur. Keep your fingers crossed.'

'I will,' she replied, holding up her crossed fingers for Jerry to see.

Jerry checked his watch:

'Oh, I better go. Call you later.'

They kissed, then Jerry climbed out of bed and left in a hurry. Maureen was left feeling content and happy. She smiled to herself while stroking her hand over her stomach - and unborn child.

8:15AM

Bat had just woken up and was sitting slouched on the edge of his bed yawning and scratching his head - still half asleep. He was dressed in his usual night attire, consisting of a white string vest and matching Y-front underpants, not the most flattering look for a man of his rounded proportions, but Bat didn't care, he was 'single and it felt comfortable' – the very words he unashamedly told his previous girlfriend, in a relationship that strangely didn't last very long. The curtains were drawn and Bat wasn't wearing his glasses, a sure-fire recipe for disaster under normal circumstances, but Bat had an almost regimented morning dress routine that he could practically do with his eyes closed – which some would argue, without his glasses, was just as good as dressing with his eyes closed.

He slowly stood up and stretched his back out straight, then dragged his feet over to a wardrobe and opened the door. Hanging up were a long line of black polo-necked shirts – all identical. Bat pointlessly rummaged through them trying to decide which one to wear. He picked one out from the middle, looked at it for a second, then shook his head and replaced it. He picked out another and held it up. He smiled approvingly – but quickly changed his mind and put it back.

Fifteen minutes later Bat was finally fully dressed and putting on his black leather jacket. The curtains were now open and bright sunshine filled the room. He stood in front of a full-length mirror and took a good long look. His polo-neck shirt was inside-out and back-to-front, a white label clearly visible under his chin. He looked curiously at himself in the mirror, but promptly switched expressions to his tough and intimidating look – something he practised frequently in front of the mirror. On this occasion he admired his evil look with satisfaction, as he recalled the last time he used it…

Bat stomped through a new housing estate located just on the outskirts of Buntleyford village. He was stubbornly in denial about his fading eyesight, and the thick lens glasses he was wearing were making little

difference; but he walked with confidence, as though he knew every brick of the estate. He was focused and determined, every stride had purpose - Bat was a man on a mission. He cunningly approximated which door he needed to call on by carefully counting each individual house he passed from the beginning of the road – a technique that seemed to be working well for him. Soon he was satisfied that he had reached his target, and marched over to the front door.

He stood on the doorstep, with scrunched eyes and a contorted face, examining the giant door number – marked 23. He produced the list given to him by Dealer on the torn piece of paper and, with the same contorted face, scrutinised the number written in large bold letters – 23. But Bat was struggling. He looked back at the door, then back at the paper, then held the paper up against the door number and compared the two – they vaguely appeared the same, so he was satisfied:

'78.....Bingo!'

He knocked long and loud on the door with a clenched fist, then loosened his shoulders ready for action. After short while the door opened. Bat was in fighting mode, he looked as hard as nails:

'William? William Jason Holland?' he demanded aggressively.

Standing at the door was William's 74-year-old

grandmother - a sweet little old lady with a soft warm voice. She was totally baffled:

'Err...no,' she said, waving a hand in front of Bat's face.

Bat flinched at the sound of the voice, and suddenly became extremely pleasant and polite. He smiled:

'Oh, sorry love, is William there please?'

'Hold on a second.'

Granny turned back inside:

'William, dear, it's for you!'

19-year-old local hooligan William Holland appeared at the door. He was slightly apprehensive at the sight of Bat:

'Yeah?' he said with attitude.

Bat slipped back into his tough guy mode:

'William? William Jason Holland?'

'Who wants to know?' replied William, acting the cocky know-it-all teenager that he was.

Bat calmly checked to his right, and then to his left – the coast was clear, or so he thought. He suddenly launched himself at William grabbing him by the shirt and throwing him outside like a rag doll. William's next-door neighbours, who had just returned home carrying an assortment of shopping bags, were standing on their doorstep watching with mouths agape.

Later that afternoon, two 16-year-old lads, Zig and Mez, were putting the finishing touches to their giant graffiti on a six-foot garden wall. Zig was armed with a yellow aerosol spray can, while Mez was spraying with a vibrant red. A final quick squiggle and the boys were done. They stepped back to admire their artwork, and were delighted; they had sprayed their tags in enormous bold capital letters. After a quick 'high five' slap in the air, they turned to run, but suddenly stopped dead in their tracks – a strange cross-eyed man dressed in black was blocking their exit.

Bat stood his ground wearing his rehearsed evil grin. His eyes were glazed - he looked verging on psychopathic. Bat slowly shook his head:

'Tut, tut, tut,' he said patronisingly. 'Even I can fuckin' see that *bastard.'*

Zig and Mez looked at each other with uncertainty, then looked back at Bat. They didn't have time to react, Bat grabbed the boys and pinned them up against the wall.

Bat leant in towards the mirror for a better look at himself. Something was troubling him. He licked his fingers and pressed down some hair that wasn't even sticking out - job done! He had completely overlooked the inside-out, back-to-front, polo shirt, but was now satisfied with his appearance, and stuck his thumbs up in approval. He produced his glasses from within his jacket and finally decided to put them on just as he was about to venture out.

8:18AM

Jeff Flowers was in bed next to his sleeping wife Anne. He had been awake for most of the night, lying motionless on his side and deep in thought. Jeff was an honest and hardworking family man, working shifts in a nearby factory for what was regarded as a fairly average London wage. His irregular working hours meant that his sleeping patterns were erratic, often finding himself wide-awake in the middle of the night. But on this particular morning his insomnia was due to anxiety...

It was late evening when Jeff answered the front door to his semidetached home in North London. He didn't normally get late callers, and was surprised to see his younger brother Scott. It had been several months since he had last seen or heard from him, and his turning up out of the blue like this, at such a late

hour, usually meant that Scott had a hidden agenda.

Scott was upbeat and happy to see his brother:

'Jeff! How are ya?'

Jeff was not at all happy to see him:

'Alright Scott,' he said, with no enthusiasm.

'You gonna invite me in then?'

After taking a moment to consider, Jeff reluctantly moved aside and Scott entered, placing a friendly hand on his brother's shoulder as he passed. He walked straight through to the lounge where Jeff's wife Anne was seated watching TV. She was pleased to see Scott and instantly rose to greet him:

'Hello Scott, long time no see.'

'Anne! How ya doing?'

Scott gave his sister-in-law a kiss followed by a big hug, while Jeff stood near the doorway and watched with his back pressed up against the wall.

'I'm fine,' said Anne. 'Can I get you a cuppa?'

'Love one,' replied Scott.

As Anne left, Scott looked over to his brother, who was still acting coldly towards him.

'What's up Jeff?' asked Scott with a smile. 'You don't look happy to see me.'

'I'm just wondering how much this visit's gonna cost me,' explained Jeff, clearly speaking from experience.

Scott made light of the comment, and laughed:

'What? I just thought I'd come over and see my brother and his family, you know?'

'Bollocks, Scott, the only time you ever turn up here, is to borrow fuckin' money. So how much?'

Scott was affronted:

'It's not like that, Jeff, I really wanted to see you,' he tried to explain.

'You still gambling, Scott?'

'I have the occasional flutter,' replied Scott hesitantly.

Jeff laughed. 'Occasional flutter?' he mocked.

'Look, Jeff, I've just come here to see you and Anne, and my little nephew. That's all.'

Scott produced a small neatly wrapped package from within his jacket:

'I even got a pressie for little Kev.'

Jeff was still not convinced - he looked at Scott with suspicion and said nothing. Scott didn't know what more he could say - he suddenly felt uncomfortable and unwelcome, he put the present down on the sofa:

'Perhaps I better go. Sorry Jeff,' he said, and headed for the door.

Jeff looked at the present - it wasn't something that Scott would normally bring, and Jeff was suddenly immersed in guilt:

'Scott,' he reluctantly called, knowing he may

regret it.

Scott stopped at the doorway and turned to face his brother.

'Look,..er... I'm sorry,' stumbled Jeff, too ashamed to look his brother in the eyes. 'Stay and have a cup of tea with us,' he continued, holding his brother's shoulder.

Scott forced a smile:

'Thanks bruv.'

Jeff was restless. His brother's visit still playing on his mind, he sensed that all was not well. A letter that had arrived for Anne in the mail the previous day was also niggling at him - when Anne opened it she seemed anxious to hide it from him. Though he found it odd, Jeff didn't question her at the time; he thought he was in a very trusting relationship and, up until then, believed that there were no secrets between them. But her behaviour was out of character and he felt compelled to investigate. Without disturbing Anne, who was still sound asleep, Jeff quietly climbed out of bed.

8:20AM

A hot day had been forecast and it was already a very warm morning. 27-year-old Quinton Verani was wide awake - lying on his king-size, silver framed bed, his bed sheets pulled down to his waist, a chrome ceiling fan rotating above him keeping him comfortably cool. Although the curtains were drawn, Quinton's east facing bedroom was brightly lit. Quinton always enjoyed waking to his surroundings - a top Italian interior designer had been flown in from Milan especially for the décor of his luxury home, every piece of furniture was meticulously selected, and very expensive. He lay on his back with hands interlocked behind his head, smiling as he remembered...

Quinton was shopping in a very upmarket jewellers. Janet, the attractive sales assistant, handed

a small bag over to him:

'Excellent choice, Mr Verani,' she said with a smile. 'I'm sure she will be over the moon.'

Quinton returned the smile:

'Thank you... fingers crossed,' he said apprehensively.

Janet crossed her fingers for Quinton to see, then watched as Quinton left for his date. As the door closed behind him, she let out a heavy sigh:

'Lucky, bitch,' she said to herself longingly.

The reality was that Quinton could make most women swoon without even having to try. With his olive skin and green eyes, his striking good looks had a rugged edge that wouldn't look out of place in a Calvin Klein poster campaign. He was stylish and often wore designer clothes, but looked equally as good in a tatty pair of jeans and a T-shirt. Quinton also owned two fancy sports cars; luxuries he could afford and had worked hard for – he was a very successful (and legitimate) businessman. Although born and raised in England, Quinton's parents were Italian, and locally Quinton was pretty much regarded as an Italian stud - wherever he went, heads would turn and women would gape.

A short while later, Quinton pulled up sharply in

his metallic royal blue convertible Mercedes sports car at a picturesque public park. He quickly exited the car and headed off across the grass. There was a spring in his step, and an air of confidence about him.

As Quinton walked, he noticed an attractive woman heading towards him. 22-year-old Caroline Carter was taking her regular shortcut through the park on her way to work. She was distracted by Quinton's good looks, and had deliberately slowed down so she could gawp:

'Wow,' she thought to herself.

She had strolled through the park many times and had never seen anything quite as stunning as Quinton.

Caroline had practically come to a standstill by the time Quinton had reached her. What she thought looked good from a distance, looked absolutely gorgeous close up and her heart rate increased. She smiled warmly hoping Quinton would notice her - Quinton didn't break stride, but had noticed and politely smiled back as he passed. Unable to take her eyes off him, Caroline about-turned and slowly walked backwards, ogling Quinton's toned physique heading away from her. She let out a lustful sigh:

'Phwooar.'

She was drifting in another galaxy when she turned back around to continue her journey and - SMACK! - walked headfirst into a tree and collapsed in a heap *on the ground.*

Moments later Quinton had reached the pond area of the park, and up ahead he could see the figure of a young woman seated on a park bench. He veered off course and purposely approached her from behind...

Quinton's reminiscing was interrupted by a loud alarm clock ringing. He reached out to the bedside cabinet and hit the alarm off - *WHACK!*

8:22AM

Dealer emerged from his house clutching the 'letter' - which had sparked off the most fearful and anxious feelings he had felt in a long time. He rushed to his Range Rover, parked in the driveway of his front garden, quickly unlocked it and threw open the door. But as he was about to step in, he suddenly stopped – the sight of the Range Rover prompting him to remember a recent meeting…

It was the early hours of the morning, and Dealer's Range Rover could be seen parked outside 'Cougars' nightclub, just off a main road in the East-End of London. The club used to be a regular haunt for Dealer, before he settled for the rural life, and he would often be seen drinking there in the evening (usually running to all hours of the morning), as many as four or five times a week – evenings that Bolt didn't

particularly enjoy as he was principally there in his capacity to protect Dealer and saw him as being an easy and vulnerable target at the club. Bolt was constantly on his guard, unsettled and on edge. Dealer on the other hand was always blasé about being out in public, he loved the attention and wasn't going to give it up that easily. Besides, as far as he was concerned he had Bolt to watch his back, and Dealer trusted him implicitly; with the exception of a few minor skirmishes throughout the years at 'Cougars', Dealer had never encountered any serious or life threatening situations, so why should he worry? But if the truth be known, it was purely down to the quick thinking and ingenuity of Bolt that Dealer had escaped many sticky situations – more often than not, situations that Dealer wasn't aware of because he was wasted from too much booze.

Whenever he could, Dealer liked to return to 'Cougars' to hook up with a few old friends and down a drink or two.

On this particular night, he had arranged a business meeting, and had been inside chatting for several hours. He concluded the meeting and was ready to leave. Bolt and Bat emerged from the club first, to check if the coast was clear before allowing Dealer to exit – something that Bolt did instinctively. There wasn't anyone in sight – Tuesday nights were always quiet, a far cry from the heaving crowds of the weekend - even the doorman had temporarily left his position for a cigarette break.

'I don't like it,' said Bat with concern, checking in all directions.

Bolt was bemused, he stood watching Bat straining to see through the darkness, and sarcastically wondered what he had done to deserve such a 'wise and learned' friend:

'You don't like what?' asked Bolt wearily.

Bat's eyes panned hard to the right, then over to the left:

'I'm still sober,' he replied with distress.

Bolt turned away, irritated. He signalled the 'all clear' to inside the club, and Dealer emerged, looking slightly the worse for drink, with an arm around his old friend Scott Flowers.

'Nice one, Scotty,' said Dealer, 'another sound deal. I dunno where ya keep findin' 'em, but I'm fuckin' glad you do, old son.'

Scott was a spiv and one of the best around - he seemed to be able to lay his hands on just about anything going – usually at short notice, and often 'to order'. Scott didn't really care what he dealt in either, hence his reputation grew rapidly within the gangster circle and he quickly became a favourite with many London villains. Dealer had a soft spot for Scott, their relationship went back a long way, to a time when Scott had lost both his dad and his wife to cancer within months of each other. Dealer had the utmost respect for Scott who had devoted his whole life to caring for his loved ones. It had been a difficult and soul-destroying time for Scott, and Dealer went out of his way to help him find his feet again. He treated Scott like a younger brother, and Scott was eternally grateful.

'Cheers, Dealer,' said Scott humbly. 'Actually, I got something else brewin' on the horizon.'

'Go on...' said Dealer, intrigued.

'How does a couple of Picasso's sound?' said Scott.

Bat overheard. 'Ooo I'd love a coffee,' he remarked.

Dealer stopped and turned to face Scott. 'You're fuckin' jokin'?'

'I kid you not,' replied Scott with a sly smile. 'They're extremely hot - the 'owner' has to get shot of them.'

'Send 'em my way, Scotty,' said Dealer with excitement.

'Yeah, seven sugars in mine,' said Bat, still desperate for a caffeine fix.

Bolt tutted and grabbed Bat by the shoulder:

'Come on,' he said, pulling him towards the car.

Scott suddenly felt anxious and somewhat awkward:

'Dealer, look, I don't like asking...' he said tentatively.

'What's up, Scotty?' asked Dealer with concern. 'You can talk to me.'

Scott paused a moment, waiting for Bolt and Bat to climb into the Range Rover - out of earshot, then continued:

'It's a bit embarrassing,' he explained softly, 'but I'm a bit short of cash.'

'Fuck's sake, Scotty, we're mates. All ya gotta do is ask,' said Dealer - peeved that Scott couldn't come straight out with it. Dealer removed a small wad of cash from within his jacket. 'A ton keep ya goin'?'

'Actually...' said Scott sheepishly, 'couldn't make it a gee, could ya?'

Dealer was concerned. He looked Scott straight in the eyes:

'You're not in any kinda trouble are ya, Scotty?'

'No, no, nothin' like that,' replied Scott dismissively.

'I hope not. You know you can come to me if you are?'

'I know that. Thanks,' said Scott sincerely.

Dealer momentarily hesitated, he kept looking at Scott for telltale signs, but Dealer had been drinking and he was aware that the alcohol wasn't helping his

*normally sound judgement. He decided to give Scott
the benefit of the doubt, after all, Scott was a valued
and very dear friend. He started counting out the
cash:*

*'Tell ya what, Scotty, consider it an advance on the
paintings.'*

*'Cheers Dealer, you're a real pal,' said Scott with
relief.*

*Dealer slapped the money into Scott's hand, and
gave him a couple of playful slaps across the cheek.
He then turned and headed towards the waiting Range
Rover:*

*'Now ya won't fuckin' forget!' he shouted over his
shoulder.*

'No chance,' replied Scott.

*Bolt, who was in the driving seat, leant across and
swung the passenger door open for Dealer as he saw
him approach.*

Dealer stood motionless in his front garden, poised
with the Range Rover's door open. His reminiscing
was interrupted by a glimpse of the 'letter' in his
hand. He instantly snapped out of his trance-like state,

and resumed his mad rush. He quickly climbed into his car and slammed the door shut.

8:25AM

The bright morning sunshine beamed through a partially open curtain angelically lighting up 24-year-old Sally Dempsey, as she lay asleep in her bed. Her eyes slowly opened and she smiled blissfully as she remembered that it was to be biggest day of her life...

It was a sunny afternoon and Sally was sitting alone on a park bench, extremely agitated and fed up that her date was late. She sat with her elbows on her knees and her chin in her hands, only lifting her head to check her wristwatch – which she seemed to be doing every few seconds. She checked her mobile phone – no messages or missed calls, her date hadn't even bothered trying to contact her. She was beginning to boil over.

From out of nowhere Quinton silently crept up

behind her, then, for no discernible reason, covered her eyes with his hands. Big mistake. Sally was up like a shot:

'*FUCK OFF, PERVERT!*' she screamed, swinging around and unleashing a vicious right hook - SMACK! - it connected sweetly with Quinton's chin, his eyes rolled back and he slowly collapsed backwards - out cold. Sally put her hands over her mouth in horror:

'Quinton!!' she screamed.

A few minutes later Sally was kneeling on the grass with Quinton's head in her lap, he was slowly coming to. Sally was extremely concerned and riddled with guilt, she continually stroked and kissed his forehead.

'Quinton, I'm sorry, I'm so sorry.'

'That's okay, my sweet...,' said Quinton, dazed and confused. '...What happened?'

'You scared the living shit out of me, that's what happened,' explained Sally.

'Did I?.... That's nice.'

'No, it's not nice. For goodness' sake, Quinton, you're supposed to say 'Guess who?' - or something like that.'

'I'm sorry, my love..,' said Quinton, still in cloud cuckoo land. 'Can I call you back? There's someone on the other line.'

'Ohh poor baby,' said Sally, cradling his head into her bosom.

15 minutes later Sally and Quinton were nestling together on the park bench. But for a rather sore jaw, Quinton seemed to have recovered from his knockout blow. He had an arm around Sally, whilst at the same time waggling his painful chin with his free hand.

'Still hurt?' asked Sally coyly.

'Naaaa...barely touched me,' said Quinton grimacing.

'Yeah, right..... So, why were you so late?'

'Sorry, I had to stop and pick something up.'

'Oh yeah?' asked Sally suspiciously.

'Yeah,' replied Quinton, with no intention of giving anything away.

'Anything important?' pursued Sally.

'Mmmm possibly,' Quinton replied nonchalantly.

Sally waited a moment for Quinton to continue, but he wasn't forthcoming:

'Well, are you gonna tell me, or do I have to smack you in the mouth again?' she said, playfully showing him her fist.

'Okay, I'll tell you, I'll tell you,' panicked Quinton.

He tapped Sally on the shoulder with the arm he had around her. Sally turned - in Quinton's hand was a ring box. She grabbed it and jumped up with *nervous excitement:*

'AHHH!! Is this what I think it is?'

'I don't know. What do you think it is?'

Sally shook the box close to her ear:

'A 42 inch plasma?!' she asked, acting dumb.

'Close,' replied Quinton.

Sally slowly opened the box, and her jaw dropped when she saw the most beautiful diamond ring, with a single stone - the biggest she'd ever seen, glistening in the sunlight.

'Oh wow,' said Sally, mesmerised.

She gazed at the ring, admiring its beauty for several breathtaking seconds, then suddenly leapt on Quinton:

'YES! YES! YES!' she said excitedly, smothering him with kisses.

'Hang on a second,' said Quinton struggling to contain her, 'I haven't popped the question yet!'

'Well, the answer's still yes!' she insisted. 'Yes, yes, yes!' and continued smothering him with kisses.

'No, no, no...you don't understand,' said Quinton turning serious. He struggled free and stood up. 'It's not you I need to pop the question to!'

'Oh,' puzzled Sally.

That evening Quinton was down on one knee trembling:

'Sir,' he said nervously, 'I wish to marry your sister, Sally, and I have come to ask for your permission...and for your blessing.'

Quinton took Dealer's hand and kissed it. Dealer looked on, absolutely mortified:

'He thinks I'm Marlon fuckin' Brando!' he said in disbelief to Sally, who was standing behind Quinton smirking.

Sally shrugged her shoulders and smiled, indicating that she had nothing to do with Quinton's performance.

Dealer suddenly slapped Quinton hard across the head with his free hand - WHACK!

'Get off!' he growled, and quickly snatched his hand back.

'OW!...Sorry,' said Quinton, bemused and unsure what he had done wrong.

'Stand up, for fuck's sake!' ordered Dealer.

Quinton quickly got to his feet, rubbing his sore head. Dealer took a second to calm himself:

'Look, Quinton, this is really simple,' he explained, 'whatever makes my sister happy, makes me happy. Do you love Sally?'

'Yes, Sir, with all my heart,' replied Quinton earnestly.

'And do you love Quinton?' he asked his sister.

'Oh yes,' she replied, wearing a radiant smile.

'And do ya both wanna get married?' Dealer asked the pair.

'Yes!' came the reply in unison.

'Then stop kissin' my fuckin' arse and get married!' finished Dealer.

Sally and Quinton embraced with excitement, Quinton lifting her off her feet and swinging her around in a full circle. After a long kiss, Quinton released his bride-to-be and approached Dealer, he was overcome with emotion:

'Dealer, I don't know what to say,' he said, reaching for Dealer's hand again.

Dealer pulled it away:

'Uh uh,' he said, showing a stern finger to indicate no kissing. Then Dealer smiled. 'Come 'ere,' he said, and gave Quinton a big hug. 'I like ya, Quinton, you're a good decent lad,' said Dealer warmly.

'Thank you, Dealer. I'll take good care of Sally.'

'I know ya will,' said Dealer, who pulled away to approach his sister.

Sally held out her hand - showing off her engagement ring:

'Look at this, Dan!' she said proudly.

Dealer was shocked: 'Fuck me!' he exclaimed. 'Must 'ave cost a fortune!'

'Nothing's too much for my Sally,' said Quinton assuredly.

'You picked a right winner there, girl,' said Dealer, very impressed indeed.

'I know,' replied Sally smugly.

Dealer hugged his sister: 'Congratulations, sis,' he said. 'Just leave everythin' to me, it'll be the best weddin' ever.'

'Luv you bruv, you're the greatest.'

'I know that,' said Dealer jokingly.

'Just one thing,' continued Sally.

'What's up?' asked Dealer.

'Who the hell is that?!'

Everyone's attention was drawn to the corner of the room, where Jimmy Todd was still bound, gagged and on his knees, with tears rolling down his cheeks. Dealer approached Jimmy and pulled the gag away:

'Well, what do ya say then?' asked Dealer sternly.

Jimmy thought for a second - he knew he had to choose his words carefully:

'Congratulations,' he winced to the engaged couple.

Quinton and Sally looked at Jimmy in bewilderment.

'Thanks,' they replied simultaneously.

73

Sally was on cloud nine as she lay in her bed. She stretched out with an ecstatic smile, and looked over to where her wedding dress hung, ready for her big day.

8:26AM

Scott Flowers had been up all night, and had only just staggered home to his penthouse apartment overlooking the river Thames in London's Waterloo. He looked rough and exhausted but there was no time to sleep, as he had an important engagement to keep.

He wandered into the kitchen and put some coffee on the boil, then dragged his feet to the bathroom for a quick shower.

10 minutes later Scott emerged from the shower wrapped in a bathrobe, his face still dripping with water. He returned to the kitchen to where the freshly made coffee pot sat simmering; the aroma triggered memories of how the previous day had begun…

Scott had met up with his old friend Jerry Coe in the restaurant of the Savoy Hotel London. This wasn't

a regular haunt of Jerry's but he'd been there several times, accompanying Donald to 'business' meetings, so he had no problem booking a table, and most of the staff knew him by name. If the truth be known, it wasn't Jerry's sort of place at all, he would much rather be sitting in a greasy builders' café drinking tea from a chipped mug - but what he was carrying that day warranted safer surroundings.

As they mulled over what they both thought was a very pretentious breakfast menu, a waiter served them with a pot of freshly ground coffee. Scott wasn't a big fan of fancy food, he briefly studied the menu choices and screwed his face up in bewilderment:

'Couldn't do us a bacon sarnie, could ya?' he asked.

The waiter frowned at the order, clearly insulted, then turned to Jerry:

'And for you, Mister Coe?'

'Yeah, make it two,' said Jerry, smirking.

The waiter was unimpressed:

'Yes Sir,' he reluctantly agreed, and began to walk away.

'Don't forget the brown sauce!' shouted Scott, to annoy the waiter further.

The waiter chose to ignore Scott and continued to the kitchen, leaving Scott and Jerry tittering like school kids.

Jerry reached under the table and produced a bulky envelope, which he slid across the table to Scott.

'Nice one, Jez,' said Scott.

Jerry was still concerned:

'24 hours is all you got, Scotty.'

'Don't worry. This time tomorrow you'll be 25 grand better off,' assured Scott with a wink.

Jerry smiled, he trusted Scott - it was all looking good.

Later that evening, Scott had made his way to a West-End London casino. He looked apprehensive as he sat himself down at a busy roulette table.

From under his jacket Scott produced the bulky envelope that Jerry had given him, and placed it on the table in front of him. He stared at it long and hard, his conscience eating away at him, he was torn - on one side was his good friend Jerry who had entrusted him with the money expecting to see a return - on the other side was the harsh reality of his huge debts, way beyond the 100 gees in the envelope; Scott was on the verge of losing everything he owned, and he saw gambling as the only way out.

Then he thought about Donald Kelly, the biggest problem of all, an uncompromising gangster to whom the cash belonged – Scott dwelt on the possible consequences should he not return the money. He was in turmoil, physically shaking. He looked around and snapped his fingers at a passing waitress, who approached.

'Whiskey – double,' he ordered, then turned back to the table.

Although the scales were finely balanced with Scott's mixed emotions, the bottom line was that his brother Jeff was right – Scott was a big-time addicted gambler; a habit that had got him into serious debt in the first place, and a habit that had undoubtedly got out of control.

There was another moment's hesitation as Scott watched the game in progress, then he cracked. He pulled a wad of cash from the envelope and slapped it down in front of the croupier:

'Chips,' requested Scott, knowing there would be no turning back.

After a brief moment, a huge pile of chips were pushed in his direction, and Scott wasted no time in strategically placing them on his 'lucky' numbers.

Two hours later, Scott was still at the table, his shirt buttons undone, sweating and distraught as his pile of chips had dwindled down to the last few. The bulky envelope was now empty. Scott's hands were trembling as he knocked back another double whiskey, and placed the last of his chips on the table.

'No more bets,' announced the croupier, and spun the wheel.

Scott's heart was pounding hard as the croupier released the ball. He watched it swirl around the wheel for what seemed like an eternity. He was worried, it was crunch time - it was all or nothing:

'Come on, come on,' he said, pleading with the wheel. It felt like everything was moving in slow motion - the ball bounced several times as the wheel slowed, before finally coming to rest on a number:

'17 Red', announced the croupier.

Scott buried his head in his hands, then suddenly threw his arms in the air with a rush of adrenaline:

'YESSSSSS!!!!!!!!!' he screamed jubilantly.

His fellow gamblers watched in envy, as four huge piles of chips were pushed towards him. He clenched a handful and kissed them.

Scott was transfixed on the coffee pot when a magpie landed on the windowsill outside, diverting his attention and snapping him out of his dreamy state. He was aware of the superstition that a single magpie symbolised bad luck, and was in two minds whether to salute it - to encourage 'good luck' (as the myth goes). The magpie's visit was brief, and it flew away before Scott had decided. He looked at the digital clock on his cooker and, realising the time, quickly poured out a mug of black coffee and carried it to the bedroom. As he entered, he stopped at the doorway and smiled with satisfaction - there were four huge piles of cash neatly stacked on his bed: Magpie or no magpie, Scott felt that luck was on his side.

8:30AM

Dealer was speeding his Range Rover through Buntleyford village. He kept glancing across to the 'letter' resting on the passenger seat – the contents still clearly disturbing him.

As he raced, he noticed the village hall up ahead…

It was early evening, and a crowd of over 70 Buntleyford folk had gathered for their monthly meeting at the village hall. Seated on the stage facing the public assembly were the village committee: The Mayor - a short, balding and tubby man pushing 70, with several double chins and a handlebar moustache. His extra body weight, coupled with his love of real ale, resulted in him always being red-faced and a tad out of breath when he spoke. He also had the problem of being excessively sweaty, and would frequently mop

his face with a handkerchief. Although the Mayor was rather pompous, his heart always seemed to be in the right place, and he did have genuine concern for the village. Sitting next to the Mayor was 65-year-old local Councillor, Janet Short – an ex school mistress, who would never tolerate unruly behaviour in her classroom and viewed the village crime problem with the same contempt. Councillor Short was not an outspoken person, but she certainly wasn't on the committee to make up the numbers, as she felt passionate about the village and all its affairs. Sitting alongside Janet was the Minister, who Chaired the village meeting, and next to him sat Councillor Neil Plummer MP – a slick, self-motivated and uncompromising man. 45-year-old Plummer had deep roots in the village, he was as sharp as a tack, and had been a respected solicitor for over ten years, working for the Crown Prosecution Service, before entering into politics. With parliamentary weight behind him, Plummer was a very powerful man, and tended to pull most of the strings in Buntleyford.

Standing at the front of the stage, at a mic'd up podium, was Betty Samuels midway through her talk. Dealer, Bolt and Bat stood together at the rear of the hall listening with interest.

Betty referred to her notes:

'...and with the £2254 we managed to raise at the

village summer fete, that gives us a running total of £7643.'

There was a warm round of applause from the attendees, then Betty summarised:

'Still a way to go to reach our target of £20,000 to renovate the recreational hall, but we're getting there.'

Betty gathered her notes together and re-seated herself.

The Minister stepped up to the podium:

'Thank you, Betty. Yes, it would be nice to finally give our restless youths somewhere to go in an evening,' he said in support. 'Which brings us nicely onto the small matter of the increasing crime problem in our village.' His mood suddenly changing.

Dealer smiled broadly, this was the part he had been waiting for. The Minister continued:

'I'm afraid we've had several complaints about the way we seem to be tackling this problem,' he said, as he looked down at the front row of the crowd, where the beaten and humiliated figure of tearaway Jimmy Todd sat with band-aids on his chin and cheek.

As the Minister's eyes panned across to the next seat, he observed the badly battered and bruised face of hooligan William Holland, followed by the beaten and battered faces of joy-riders Sean and Frederick. The following 10 seats were entirely taken up by local hooligan teenagers, all battered, bruised, bloodied and distraught. Graffiti boys, Zig and Mez, were seated together at the end of the row looking shell-shocked – Zig's face and hair had been completely sprayed red, and Mez's completely yellow.

Although the Minister was alarmed at the scary sight of the misguided teenagers, now resembling the cast from 'The Rocky Horror Picture Show', he was more concerned at the manner in which the youth crime problem was being tackled. The lawlessness of it all was getting to him.

Councillor Short and the Mayor glanced across at each other and discreetly smiled, while Councillor Plummer - who didn't condone violence - somehow managed to hide his anger, even though he was infuriated by the state of the teenagers.

'I think our interpretation of 'aving a quiet word', *' said the Minister with a mock cockney accent, 'may be somewhat different to others.'*

Dealer, Bolt and Bat smugly smiled. Dealer put an unlit cigar to his mouth.

Christopher Dingle suddenly stood up:

'Who cares about the interpretation?' he shouted. 'Crime seems to have fallen overnight!'

Several cries of 'here, here,' echoed through the hall. Then the Colonel stood up:

'They're animals, you know! All stinking, rotten,

filthy bitches! The lot of them!'

'Well said, Colonel,' shouted Mrs Watts – also relieved that the Colonel had remembered his trousers on this occasion.

'As much fun as it all appears to be...' said the Minister firmly, '...especially with the paint,' he sniggered, 'we can't just take the law into our own hands, Mrs Watts.'

Christopher perked up again:

'Nonsense!' he bellowed. 'A good old fashioned slap never hurt my kids!'

'That's 'cause you weren't slapping the buggers hard enough!' insisted the Colonel with authority.

The villagers laughed, and Mrs Watts stood up:

'Frankly Vicar, as long as it's safe to walk the streets at night, I, for one, don't care how the problem is dealt with.'

Her comment invoked a rapturous round of applause, which made Mrs Watts feel quite heroic for her outburst, she coyly adjusted her hair and took a little bow - milking the attention. The Mayor turned to the Councillors and sheepishly nodded in agreement with Mrs Watts' comment. This didn't sit well with Councillor Plummer who gave the Mayor a disapproving look. The Mayor suddenly felt uneasy, he nervously adjusted his tie and mopped his sweating brow with a hanky.

The Minister was beginning to feel overpowered and out-numbered. He twirled a gold ring on his finger – a nervous habit that he had:

'Mister Dempsey!...' he shouted across the hall, over the noise of the crowd. 'I don't suppose you would care to contribute anything to this discussion... at all?' he continued, with little hope of a response.

Dealer removed the cigar from his mouth:

'Yeah...,' he replied, prompting silence in the hall.

The Minister was surprised:

'Well, kiss my ring,' he mumbled to himself, 'here's a first.'

All eyes turned towards Dealer in silent anticipation.

'What time's the bar open?' asked Dealer.

'Here, here!' hollered the Colonel.

'Good idea,' agreed the Mayor, mopping his brow again.

'And there speaketh the thirsty,' said the Minister, exasperated.

The Mayor was up on his feet:

'Yes, I think that concludes our meeting everyone, thank you. See you next month!'

With that, the crowd began to disburse, leaving the Minister shaking his head in defeat.

Sitting in the second row was Fanny Tattle transfixed by the bright yellow and red paintwork on *the faces and hair of graffiti boys Zig and Mez:*

'Oh yeah,' she remembered with a deadpan expression. 'Never buy a house next to traffic lights.'

A short while later, the village folk had gathered at the bar area of the hall. Bolt and Bat watched as the Minister shook Dealer's hand with vigour:

'...I'd be absolutely delighted to marry Sally and Quinton,' said the Minister, genuinely flattered. 'Thank you for asking me.'

'No, thank you, Vicar,' said Dealer.

As they shook hands, Mrs Watts approached brandishing one of her legendary home-made pies - the Minister spotted it in her hands:

'Ah, here comes a tasty looking tart...and I do believe she's holding a pie,' quipped the Minister, with his new found wit. He released Dealer's hand. 'I'll leave you to it,' he said, backing away.

Mrs Watts was all smiles as she strolled up to Dealer and his pals:

'I've baked a pie for you boys,' she said, handing it to Dealer.

'That's very kind of you, Mrs Watts,' said Dealer politely.

'It's gooseberry,' said Mrs Watts.

'Thank you, Miss Gooseberry,' said Bat gratefully.

Bolt tutted and rolled his eyes.

'I'm sure it will be delicious,' said Dealer.

'Yeah, thanks,' added Bolt with a smile.

'Just my way of saying 'thank you',' said Mrs Watts with a suggestive wink and a quick flirtatious adjustment of her hair as she walked away.

Bolt sniffed the pie and turned his nose up:

'Not really into gooseberry.'

'Na, me neither,' said Dealer.

'Ahhh come on,' said Bat defensively, 'she seemed quite nice! She made us a pie, look.'

Dealer and Bolt looked at Bat in disbelief, which made Bat feel uncomfortable.

'Well, we could always give it to Jimmy - your new dog,' said Bat, still unaware as to who Jimmy was.

Dealer slapped himself on the forehead and looked to the heavens for help.

'What?' asked Bat with a gormless smile.

Dealer ignored him – instead he turned away and set the pie down on the bar. He was just turning back when he caught sight of Councillor Plummer and stopped dead - Plummer was looking daggers at him. Dealer stood tall and stared Plummer out, there was clear friction between them. Bolt watched the stand-off with confusion, it was extremely confrontational and neither were about to back down, but Plummer was suddenly distracted by Betty who started to talk to him in her normal persistent manner, and Plummer *reluctantly backed down to respond to her.*

'What was that all about?' enquired Bolt.

'That fucker unnerves me,' replied Dealer.

Bolt laughed. 'Who, Plummer?'

'You could 'ave him for breakfast, Dan,' insisted Bat.

'See boys, that's where you've gotta lot to learn,' said Dealer regaining his composure. 'Councillor Plummer is a very, very dangerous man - and our worst enemy.'

'Why?' asked Bat, still unconvinced.

''cos he's fuckin' straight,' explained Dealer. 'He's so squeaky clean, you can hear the cheeks of his arse rubbin' together when he walks.'

Just then the Mayor approached looking purposeful and serious.

'Unlike this twat,' continued Dealer.

'Mr Dempsey,' said the Mayor, marching straight up to Dealer.

'Mayor,' replied Dealer calmly.

'Can't say I approve of this Charles Bronson, vigilante-type approach,' said the Mayor with authority.

Dealer grinned. 'No, of course you can't,' he said with heavy sarcasm.

The Mayor checked all around to ensure no one was watching or listening, then discreetly slipped a *bulky envelope, packed with cash, to Dealer.*

'...But I do believe you and I are singing from the same hymn book,' continued the Mayor with lowered voice.

Dealer raised his glass. 'All things bright and beautiful?'

'Certainly!' said the Mayor with a sly smile.

Bolt smiled and raised his glass. 'We three kings?'

'Absolutely!' replied the Mayor.

Bat suddenly jumped in and raised his glass. 'O Little Town Of Bethlehem?' he asked excitedly.

The Mayor looked at Bat in confusion. 'Yes... anyway.....,' he said, blotting his perspiring forehead with his hanky. He leant towards Dealer. 'Keep up the good work,' he said quietly with a wink. And with that, the Mayor was off.

Bat watched the Mayor waddle away, and paused for a moment deep in thought. He turned to Dealer:

'What the fuck was that all about?'

'Never mind,' replied Dealer. 'Drink up.'

At that moment, Betty approached with urgency:

'Ah Danny, caught you,' she said. 'Could I have a word?...The fundraising?'

'Oh Betty, I'd love to talk,' said Dealer condescendingly. 'But we gotta meetin' to get to.' Dealer downed his drink in one, and slammed the glass down onto the bar.

Dealer had arrived at his destination. He pulled the Range Rover over sharply into a car park next to a faded white office block, and parked up near the main doors. He turned the engine off, grabbed the 'letter' from the passenger seat, and hastily climbed from the car.

8:32AM

55-year-old Maria Verani had had a sleepless night suffering from a severe bout of anxiety. She was in her bedroom, the curtains were still drawn, and Maria, wrapped in her night-robe, was knelt at her bedside, hands clasped together in prayer. She was extremely upset, and whimpered as she quietly prayed. She clutched a silver crucifix that hung around her neck, and as she kissed it, it brought back memories...

Maria was in the living room with her only offspring – her beloved son Quinton. Maria was Italian, born and bred, and, although she had lived in London for a great number of years, she had never lost her Italian roots, nor her very broad Neapolitan accent. She was dressed typically of an Italian widow - in black, even though her husband wasn't actually

dead; he had run off with another woman, but Maria was far too proud to divulge something as demeaning as that to the neighbours – it was far more dignified and socially acceptable to say he was dead. Besides, as far as she was concerned, he was dead - and she had said it so many times she was actually beginning to believe it herself. Maria was kissing her silver crucifix and looking mortified:

'You ask' a gangster to marry you?!' she said, dumbfounded.

Quinton was sitting beside his mother on the couch, he was desperately trying to remain calm and in control, but his mother always had a way of making him feel uncomfortable. She always knew which strings to tug to keep him in line – emotional blackmail was her forte, and Quinton was henpecked to within an inch of his life.

'No, Mamma, I asked if I can marry his sister. His sister, Mamma,' pleaded Quinton.

''Ees sister is gangster?'

'No, his sister is Sally.'

'Who'da hell is Sally?!'

'Sally, Mamma: The girl I have been bringing home for the past seven months!' replied Quinton in disbelief.

'But yesterday 'was Cindy!'

'No Mamma, yesterday was Sally, today is Sally,

tomorrow will be Sally.'

Maria was baffled. '...All da same Sally?'

'Of course all the same Sally. Do you think I have a different Sally for every day of the week?'

''ow'da hell should I know, you never talk'a to your Mamma!'

Quinton slumped back in his seat and slapped his hands together, pleading with God for holy intervention.

'So, Sandie, da gangster!' continued Maria maliciously.

'No, it's Sally; and she's not a gangster.'

'And you, now you wanna be Al Pacino!'

'Oh Mamma,' said Quinton, beginning to wish he had just eloped.

Maria had tears in her eyes – a master of producing them in a heartbeat. She was suddenly calm.

'Come 'ere, my son,' she said gently, and affectionately pulled Quinton towards her. Then, in a swift change of mood, began rummaging aggressively through his hair.

'OW!' screamed Quinton. 'What are you doing!?'

'I'm'a lookin' for three 6's!'

'What?!!'

'Dey 'ere somewhere, three 6's, I know dey 'ere!!'

As Maria rotated Quinton's head, she took a split

second to examine the contents of his ear, and grimaced with disgust.

'OUCH!! You're hurting!!' yelled Quinton who managed to pull free and stand up, rubbing his head in pain. 'Mamma, there are no 6's!!'

''ow'd you know?!' said Maria. 'Do you 'ave eyes in back of 'ead?!!'

Maria suddenly drew in a sharp breath:

'Of course, it all make'a sense.' She crossed herself, and again kissed the crucifix around her neck.

'Oh Mamma,' said Quinton in despair, he knew there was no reasoning with her when she was in this sort of mood.

Maria clasped her hands together in prayer:

'Oh Lord, why you curse'a me so? Whatta 'ave I done to deserve such a wanker for a son?'

'Mamma!' said Quinton, shocked.

'Don't interrupt your Mamma, canna you see I'm praying?!'

'But you can't call me that!' insisted Quinton.

'Why not?' said Maria dismissively. 'All your friends do.'

Quinton was thrown. 'Yeah but....I mean...,' he stumbled for a reply. 'Do you know what it actually means?' he asked, banking on the fact that his mother was very naive in that respect.

'No, you tell'a your Mamma whad' it mean?'

replied Maria.

'Well...it means...sort of...,' he stumbled again, knowing he could never talk to his mother about such matters. 'I can't tell you what it means!' he suddenly blurted.

'Den you're a bigger wanker dan I t'ought you were!' concluded Maria.

'Mamma!' said Quinton, astounded at his mother's profanities.

Maria looked up to heavens in prayer, and switched to her dependable crying mode - tears instantly filling her eyes:

'He canna even speak'a to 'ees own Mamma. Me - da woman who suffer' 'ees birth, seven days in'a labour!..'

'Please Mamma..,' said Quinton, beginning to feel the guilt.

'Me, da woman 'oose 'usband run off wid a psycho slag from Sicily...'

Quinton sat on the couch near his mother. 'Mamma..,' he pleaded.

'Me, da Mamma who work'a little finger to da bone, scrubbin' an'a cleanin' an'a washin'...,' Maria continued with her charade.

'Mamma please...'

'...'ees smelly socks, 'ees'a filthy disgusting underpants...'

'Mamma don't do this...'

'..And now 'ee wanna leave me,' she said with a tremor in her voice. 'Me, 'ees poor 'elpless, defenceless Mamma...'

She burst into floods of tears and wept like a baby, her hands clasped together under her chin, her body gently rocking to and fro. It was an Oscar winning performance – and it was working a charm.

Quinton was reduced to tears - he too started crying like his mother:

'Mamma please stop,' he begged, tears rolling down his cheeks.

Still not satisfied with his reaction, Maria buried her head in her hands, and increased her wailing by several decibels.

Quinton moved in closer:

'Mamma, please,' he pleaded.

Maria slyly spread her fingers to observe Quinton - who was just out of range. Quinton was heartbroken to see his mother like this, his crying also heightened. He shuffled even closer:

'Mamma,' he wept, reaching out to try and hold her.

Close enough - Maria suddenly snapped out of her crying mode - WHACK! - she slapped Quinton hard across the face, sending him flying off the couch and onto the floor. Quinton was stunned.

'Whad' I tell you 'bout interruptin' your Mamma's prayers?!' said Maria angrily.

Quinton rubbed his cheek in pain. 'Sorry, Mamma,' he said sheepishly.

'Now go an' scrub'a your ears out!' she demanded. *'Der's more shit in 'der than Channel 5!'*

Maria looked up to the heavens in despair. 'No wonder 'ee never listens to 'ees Mamma!'

Maria was crouched in prayer. She once again kissed the crucifix clutched in her hand, and rose to get dressed for what she believed was going to be the worst day of her life – her son's wedding.

8:33AM

Councillor Neil Plummer MP was sitting up in bed smoking a cigarette while his wife lay asleep next to him. The animosity he felt for Dealer had given Plummer a restless night, and he had chain-smoked his way through the best part of it. As Plummer flicked more ash into an already brimming ashtray resting on his lap, he recalled a recent conversation...

Plummer was seated in his office at the local Town Hall opposite his secretary Timothy Dale. Plummer was vexed, he had sent Timothy out on an investigative assignment and Timothy had returned with unsatisfactory news. Plummer stubbed out a cigarette into an ashtray using unnecessary force, splitting the butt wide open:

'But he's a self confessed gangster!' erupted

Plummer, clearly irritated. 'There must be something incriminating that we can find?'

'I know he's a crook, Councillor,' explained Timothy calmly, 'but Dempsey is also a very clever man, we can't find anything.'

'What about all those kids he beat up?'

Timothy let out a sardonic laugh. 'They're not going to talk - no one is going to talk. Not only is he clever, but he is also very feared.'

Plummer got to his feet and paced to the window:

'Damn it, Tim, why did he have to move into my neighbourhood?'

Timothy shrugged his shoulders.

Plummer stood at the window deep in thought for a moment as he looked out at the view of the village he adored:

'Well, if we can't find anything on him,' he continued, 'then the least we can do is make his stay here as uncomfortable and miserable as possible.'

Plummer was plotting Dealer's downfall when his wife rolled over in bed and interrupted his train of thought. He took a final drag from his half-smoked

102

cigarette and stubbed the rest out. He then climbed out
of bed to get ready for a day at the office.

8:36AM

60-year-old Professor Philip Pringle scrambled out of bed in his shabby council home, and put on his slippers. He threw open the curtains and poked his head out of an open window into the brilliant sunshine. The warmth of the sun was exhilarating and he took in a deep breath of fresh air:

'Ahhh,' he rejoiced optimistically. 'Another day!'

Pringle was a scatty, jittery, eccentric who was completely hyperactive and seemed to have an endless supply of energy – constantly buzzing as though he was high on drugs. His intelligence was unfathomable, he was perpetually brimming with ideas and concepts, his brain never seemed to relax – this ultimately meant that he was (metaphorically speaking) always in ten different places at any one time, which tended to make him a walking time-bomb - wherever Pringle appeared, accidents seemed to follow.

Pringle quickly wrapped himself in an old dressing gown, and made his way to the kitchen where he was met by his precious, but now ageing, cat, Eros.

'Good morning Eros, old boy,' said Pringle excitedly, petting the jet-black cat with affection – stroking him under the chin and kissing him on the head. Eros was pleased to see Pringle and loved being pampered, but Eros also knew that morning time meant feeding time.

Pringle opened and explored the fridge, emerging with an opened tin of cat food. He folded back the lid - the tin was practically empty.

'Not to worry, plenty more where this came from,' he assured Eros, scraping what little food there was into Eros' cat bowl.

He discarded the empty tin, opened an eye-level cupboard, and was somewhat surprised to see the cupboard was empty.

'That's odd,' said Pringle, scratching his head. He turned to his cat:

'Sorry, Eros, it appears that's all there is,' he explained with embarrassment. He put the bowl down onto the floor and Eros immediately tucked into the minuscule amount.

'Could have sworn I bought another tin,' puzzled Pringle.

He took another look into the empty cupboard almost in disbelief, then cast his mind back to the previous day...

It was midday at the 'Strudwick Scientific Research Laboratories', and Professor Pringle was hard at work in one of the labs. He was dressed in white overalls, rubber gloves and protective goggles, and was surrounded by hi-tech scientific equipment. In all four corners of the lab there was an abundance of circuitry, beakers, compounds, tools and machinery, and it was all looking a mess. This was typical of Pringle who, in his excitement, wouldn't think twice of tearing the place apart trying to locate something he needed, and then not putting the item back once he had used it – and so the chaotic cycle continued. But many considered him a genius, so his methods in the workplace were tolerated. However, as in the case of his current employer, his methods did have a tendency to rub people up the wrong way. This was not helped by the fact that he had been working on his current project for over six months with little success. Nevertheless, Pringle was as enthusiastic as ever.

A yellow liquid bubbled in a beaker over a Bunsen burner. Pringle's brain was in hyper-drive. He turned to a giant blackboard covered with his equations, and manically rubbed out a formula; then at lightening speed chalked in a new one. He stepped back to look and was shocked, his blood ran cold. He slowly slipped the goggles up onto his forehead.

'Oh...my,' he said with a tremor, as a lump came to his throat. His eyes were fixed on the blackboard. 'Eros, old boy, I think I've cracked it.'

His lethargic cat Eros sat, completely uninterested, on a stool close by. He seemed content to just lick his paws, but the truth was, Eros probably daren't move for fear of entangling himself in the chaos that surrounded him – a lesson he had learnt from three previous visits.

Pringle was in awe of his calculation:

'Yes, yes, of course, why didn't I see this before?'

He pondered briefly, then suddenly snapped out of his trance-like state - returning to his hyper-self. He hastily made his way over to a steel hexagonal box - around 3ft squared in size - that he had constructed in the workshop. He flipped open the hinged lid - inside was a mass of electronic circuit boards, ribbons, cables and wires.

Pringle removed his gloves and dived in, pulling out a circuit board and hastily making alterations.

'A few adjustments, Eros, that's all we need!' he explained with excitement. He took a soldering iron and quickly secured his amendments, smoke pouring

from the lid as he soldered the joins.

Pringle slammed the lid shut and returned to the bubbling yellow liquid. He slid the goggles back over his eyes, pulled on his gloves, carefully added a spoon of white powdered crystals to the beaker and gently stirred. Holding the beaker up to the light, he examined the contents, then, for no scientific reason, took a quick sniff of the releasing vapours and coughed out loud.

'Delicious,' he said gruffly with sarcasm. He carried it over to the hexagonal box, unscrewed a small cap from its side, and carefully poured the beaker's contents into the hole.

'Now, if this gas can just react quickly enough... then our council house days could be over,' he said with trepidation.

Eros miaowed nonchalantly.

'Exactly,' agreed Pringle.

With the liquid poured, Pringle screwed the cap back in place, then opened a small door located in the side of the box:

'Something to put inside,' said Pringle, frantically searching all around him. 'Ah!' he exclaimed, as he spotted a tin of cat food that he had bought that morning.

He placed the tin inside the box, closed the door and secured it with four silver latches. He walked over to a giant electrical lever located on the wall and placed both hands upon it, ready to pull. Pringle was breathing erratically – excited, yet apprehensive. He turned to his cat:

'Paws crossed, Eros,' he said. And with that, pulled the lever down to activate the power.

A loud electrical hum filled the lab, and Eros sat up alert. Smoke began to exude, and the hum became louder. Soon, electrical static flashes were emanating from the box as it started to shake.

'Yes, yes!!' Pringle cried with wild anticipation, clenching his fist and willing the machine to work.

The static rays grew more erratic, blue electrical flashes bounced off the walls and ceiling, the box shook violently - the hum was deafening. Eros was up on all fours with arched back and tail in the air.

Pringle grew more excited:

'YES, YES!' he yelled with hands held aloft, laughing psychotically at the top of his voice. At that moment, he was the 'mad scientist' - comparable to Dr Frankenstein creating his monster. Pringle turned to his cat:

'Eros! Just one word, old boy,' he bellowed like a man possessed. '...RUN!!!!'

Pringle picked up his cat and made a mad dash for the door. He threw it open and managed to get himself out into the corridor, slamming the door behind him, when there was an almighty explosion - BANG!! *The corridor shuddered, sending shock waves vibrating throughout the whole building.*

There followed a deathly silence. Pringle rested his back up against the corridor wall and let out a huge sigh of relief. Suddenly the distant sound of stomping footsteps echoed in the corridor, getting louder with every step.

'Oh shit,' said Pringle with sense of dread. He knew exactly who they belonged to, he'd heard those size 14's many times before.

They belonged to Professor Jason Strudwick, proprietor of the 'Strudwick Scientific Research Laboratories' – and Pringle's employer. Strudwick emerged into the corridor and stormed towards Pringle with a face like thunder. Strudwick was a giant of a man who towered over Pringle, and was four times his body width. On a good day Strudwick had a chilling and strangely distorted face - on a bad day he resembled a rabid dog, one snarl alone could render the average man to soil himself. This was one of those bad days - the blood drained from Pringle's face, leaving him ghostly pale from fear.

'Pringle!!' screamed Strudwick, his face as red as a beetroot. 'What the hell was that noise?!!' he demanded to know.

Pringle's body tensed as he prepared himself for

the onslaught. 'Noise, Mr Strudwick?...' he lied unconvincingly whilst quaking in his shoes. '...I didn't hear any noise.'

As Strudwick approached he spotted Eros in Pringle's arms. 'I thought I told you not to bring that giant rat to work!!' he yelled.

Pringle nervously stumbled for an excuse. 'Yes.. I know...but...err I had to take him to the vet...and I was pushed for time, and...'

'What are you doing in the corridor?!' interrupted Strudwick with suspicion.

Pringle couldn't think quickly enough. 'Oh...er...'

'What have you done to my lab, Pringle?!!'

'Lab?' replied Pringle, trying to look innocent.

Strudwick slowly edged his way over to the lab door and, without taking his eyes from Pringle's guilt-ridden face, swung the door wide open. Pringle braced himself for the worst as Strudwick poked his head inside. A few seconds later Strudwick emerged from the lab and calmly closed the door. He slowly turned to Pringle:

'YOU'RE FIRED!!'

Pringle was staring into the empty cupboard:

'Oh yes, that's what happened to it,' he said, recollecting:

'Right! Busy day ahead, Eros. I'll pick up another tin while I'm out.'

With that, Pringle left the kitchen in a hurry. Eros had finished what little food there was, he looked up and miaowed, still hungry.

8:46AM

Dealer had arrived at the work place of forensic expert John Stanton. Their acquaintance stretched way back, long before John had established himself as a leading criminal forensic investigator, and long before Dealer had earned his notorious nickname. John had always liked Dealer and was forever indebted to him for resolving a situation that was costing a lot of time, money and placing an immense amount of strain on his marriage:

John had just successfully completed four gruelling years of medical school, and had gone on a long safari trip with his wife. To their astonishment, they returned to find squatters had moved into their home and changed all the locks. After a month of having to live in a grubby bed & breakfast, and making very slow progress through the proper legal channels to repossess their home, a close friend suggested contacting local hard man Danny Dempsey - which he did reluctantly out of desperation. To his surprise he found Danny to be very approachable, good humoured and down to earth, and they seemed to hit it off from the start - Danny was happy to help out as a favour:

'Don't worry, I'll deal with it,' he said nonchalantly – words that would forever stay etched in John's memory.

That same evening, Danny and his pals busted down a back door and had the squatters out on their backsides within 10 minutes. Not only had they given them a severe hiding - just for the hell of it, but they had threatened them to the point that they wouldn't dare go to the authorities, or even think about coming back – such was Danny's reputation at the time. John got his house back, albeit with a few bloodstained carpets, courtesy of Danny's brutality, and the problem was solved.

As eternally grateful as John was to Dealer, their 'working' paths over the years couldn't have been more different. John was aware of Dealer's criminal activities and wanted to keep their association at arm's length, which, up until now, was something that Dealer understood and respected: The thought of a gangster turning up out of the blue at a forensic lab, where there was normally a strong police presence, worried John immensely and it was only by chance that Dealer had caught him at a time when he happened to be alone in the lab.

John had never seen Dealer so agitated; Dealer had arrived filled with anxiety and urgency. John had no doubt that it was important, so he invited him in, and hoped that no-one would interrupt.

Dealer couldn't relax. He stood by the window puffing on a cigar, waiting apprehensively as John sat examining the handwriting on the 'letter' under a giant magnifying glass. John readjusted the position of a brightly illuminated desk lamp and examined the 'letter' with closer scrutiny. He scrolled across to examine the handwriting on the other letter that Dealer had taken from the drawer; backwards and forwards he scanned, carefully examining both letters.

Dealer began to anxiously pace the room:

'Well?' he asked impatiently.

'Well...,' replied John, still examining, 'these two letters were written by the same person.'

'Are you absolutely sure?' asked Dealer, who was half hoping for a different answer.

'I could go through it with you, pointing out all the similarities...,' explained John, still scrutinising the handwriting.

'Could it 'ave been forged?'

John examined it further, looking at the way the S's curled and the O's looped:

'Well, if it is, then it's the best hand-written forgery

I've ever seen, and I've been in this game for 20 years.'

'But it's possible?' probed Dealer like a high court lawyer.

John put the magnifying glass down:

'Possible, but highly unlikely. Look, Danny, you wanted my expert opinion, and I say they were written by the same person.'

Dealer was stunned. He knew the analysis wasn't 100% conclusive - it was just an opinion, but an opinion Dealer valued, and it knocked him for six. He paced the room fearful of the 'letter's' contents and even more apprehensive than he was before.

After a moment of realisation that the 'letter' could just be the 'real deal', Dealer removed some cash from his wallet and stuffed it into John's breast pocket:

'Cheers John, mate. I appreciate this.'

'No problem,' said John, who was confused by what he had seen, but didn't want to know any more than he really needed to.

'Keep this under your hat,' said Dealer.

'Of course,' said John reassuringly.

Dealer collected his letters and headed for the door.

A few minutes later, Dealer emerged from the forensic building. As he hurried towards his parked

Range Rover, he folded the 'letter' and safely placed it inside his jacket. En route, his eye caught sight of a giant shutter slowly opening in a warehouse across the street. He slowed to a halt as it triggered memories...

Bolt's BMW pulled up swiftly outside a warehouse. Dealer and Bolt quickly climbed from the car and made their way to the giant shutters as they began to lift. They looked concerned as they stood watching, and soon their worst fears were confirmed when the shutters were fully open and their view of the interior unhindered. They took a few steps inside and stopped - the warehouse had been completely cleaned out.

They were approached by warehouse manager, Terry McCoy, who looked very distraught, physically shaking and worried as to how Dealer would react.

'What the fuck 'appened this time, Tel?!' asked Dealer.

'Sorry Dealer,' replied Terry, trembling, 'same routine: Old Bill came with a warrant and three trucks.'

'Fuck!' said Dealer.

'They wanted to see invoices for everythin',' explained Terry. 'When I couldn't produce 'em, they

cleaned us out.'

Dealer was baffled. 'But... we got people on the payroll for this shit not to 'appen - 'aven't we Bolt?'

Bolt was equally confused. 'Well... yeah,' he replied.

'Then 'ow the fuck can this 'appen?! To three *of our fuckin' warehouses?!' continued Dealer.*

Bolt and Terry shrugged their shoulders.

At that moment, Bat entered the warehouse in a hurry. He looked purposeful as he marched over to Dealer:

'Dealer, I think you better look at this,' he said, producing a leaflet from his pocket.

He handed it to Dealer, who scanned it with raised eyebrows:

'Viagra sale?'

'Oh.... Where did that come from?' said Bat unconvincingly. He tentatively took the leaflet back, then handed Dealer another sheet.

Dealer snatched it from his hand and read the leaflet expecting it to be as equally ridiculous – but it wasn't, Dealer read with a sense of dread.

'What is it?' asked Bolt.

'Copy of the warrant,' replied Bat.

'Nice one, Bat,' commended Bolt, impressed with Bat's ingenuity.

Dealer was utterly pissed off. 'Oh for fuck's sake,'

he said, turning away in despair, and pushing the warrant into Bolt's chest.

Bolt read the warrant with interest:

'Shit,' he said, dismayed. ''Authorised by Neil Plummer MP'.'

'Told ya he was our worst fuckin' enemy,' said Dealer.

Bolt was peeved. 'Let me take him out, Dealer,' he offered.

Bat looked perplexed. 'What...to a gay bar?'

'Shut up, Bat,' snapped Bolt. 'One bolt, Dealer, right between the eyes, and problem over!'

'No one's gonna to take anyone out, Bolt!' insisted Dealer. 'Especially an M fuckin' P!'

There was a moment's silence while Dealer thought.

'So, what are we gonna do?' wondered Bat.

'Dunno, Bat,' replied Dealer. 'But this is gonna take brains.'

Bat nodded in agreement, his eyes gazing into open space. He began stroking his chin and tapped an index finger on his lower lip.

'Hmmmmm,' said Bat in a full cartoon pose of concentration.

Dealer, Bolt and Terry watched Bat in disbelief.

'Bat,' said Dealer calmly, 'go 'n' get yer Viagra, before they sell out.'

'Right,' said Bat enthusiastically. 'Good idea.' He instantly about-turned and headed for the exit.

Dealer was still transfixed upon the shutters of a nearby warehouse - troubled and lost in his memories. A loud horn from a passing car suddenly brought him back down to Earth. It took a second to get his bearings, then he jumped into his car, started the engine and was off.

9:05AM

Jeff Flowers was seated at the breakfast table, closely studying a bank statement. He was deeply concerned.

His wife Anne, wrapped in a dressing gown, entered the kitchen and headed straight for the kettle:

'You were up early,' she said. 'Couldn't sleep?'

'No,' replied Jeff belligerently.

'What's up?' asked Anne, filling the kettle from the tap.

'This..,' said Jeff, holding out the statement.

Anne looked over and was suddenly apprehensive – she had purposely put it in a place that she thought Jeff wouldn't normally look.

'...Fifteen hundred pounds cash withdrawal,' continued Jeff gravely.

Anne's face dropped - she instantly knew:

'Oh,' she said, abandoning the kettle.

'Look, I know I said it's your account to do what you want with,' explained Jeff calmly, 'but that's a lot of money and I just want you to be honest with me.'

Anne sat next to her husband, she felt ashamed of what she had done, but also worried as to how her husband would react.

'Don't be angry Jeff,' she said hesitantly, '... but... I lent it to your brother.'

Jeff buried his head in his hands.

'He said he was desperate,' reasoned Anne. 'He was in tears.'

Jeff looked up at Anne and was angry:

'Scott's a gambler, Anne - an addicted fuckin' gambler!' he explained for the umpteenth time, annoyed that he was having to explain it again. 'He's always gonna need money! He's always gonna be desperate!'

Anne was in tears, she knew she shouldn't have lent the money, but the problem was that she was a caring person and a sucker for a hard luck story:

'I'm sorry, Jeff, I just didn't have the heart to say no. He's family,' she explained, trying to justify her actions.

A moment passed as Jeff watched his wife wipe away her tears. He felt guilty for snapping at her, because deep down he knew Anne would have had the best intentions. He took Anne's hand and held it sympathetically:

'It's okay, I don't blame you,' he said, hugging his wife.

Jeff was clearly annoyed with his brother, it was not the first time Scott had taken advantage of Anne's good nature, but he was determined that it would be the last.

11:24AM

Dealer and Bolt lay hidden in riverbank rushes. Dealer was holding a pair of binoculars and was looking out to the river, whilst Bolt was looking baffled:

'What the hell are we doin' 'ere, Dealer?' he asked with concern. 'Ain't your sister gettin' married in less than an hour?'

'We're watchin' that boat over there,' replied Dealer, nodding towards a solitary large white craft drifting alone in the middle of the river.

'Oh, I see.., that explains it,' said Bolt sarcastically, 'and that's more important than Sally's weddin', is it?'

'Where's Bat?' asked Dealer, completely blanking Bolt's question.

'He said he'll be 'ere, but let's face it, he could be any-fuckin'-where.'

'I thought he went to get his eyes sorted?'

'He did...but I think they're worse.'

'Worse! 'ow can they be fuckin' worse? He's as

blind as a bat as it is.'

'Well, I warned him, but he still went to some back street quack with a two bob laser pen,' explained Bolt.

'Idiot, I told him I'd fuckin' pay for it!' said Dealer angrily.

Dealer looked through the binoculars at the boat, the name 'OWMUTCH' clearly written on the bow. There was no sign of any movement on deck.

'So this boat.....?' enquired Bolt.

'Yeah.'

'Are we buyin' it, or somethin'?'

'No,' said Dealer bluntly. 'What's the time?'

Bolt checked his watch. 'Twenty-five past.'

'Okay, Bolt, keep watchin'. If my sources are correct, it should 'appen anytime now.'

'Sources? What the fuck are you on about?' worried Bolt.

'Shhh just keep watchin', I need you to be a witness.'

'Witness?! Witness to what?!' exclaimed Bolt.

'Shhh!' demanded Dealer.

Just then they heard Bat's voice:

'DEALER!...BOLT!' he called in a loud whisper.

Dealer and Bolt circled around to see Bat, with his thick lens glasses, wandering aimlessly in the rushes.

'Over here, Bat!' cried Bolt, trying not to shout.

'Where? I can't see ya,' said Bat with frustration,

looking in all directions.

Dealer shook his head in dismay:

'Go and get him, before he ends up in the fuckin' river,' he said gruffly to Bolt.

Bolt tutted as he reluctantly got to his feet, and scurried off to get Bat.

A moment later Bolt returned dragging Bat by the shoulder to where Dealer lay.

'Alright, Dealer, 'ow are ya?!' said Bat overzealously.

'Shut up and get down!' ordered Dealer.

'Sorry, Dan,' whispered Bat, and quickly hit the floor. But it wasn't long before he got excited again. 'Are we bird watchin' then?'

'Bird watchin'?' said Bolt in disbelief.

Bat was clearly puzzled:

'Fish watchin'?' he offered as the only feasible alternative that sprang to mind.

'Oh don't be a prat all your life, Bat,' snapped Bolt.

'What are we watchin' then?' asked Bat, bemused.

'Just belt up, and keep yer eyes on that boat,' said Dealer, nodding towards the 'OWMUTCH'.

'Got ya!' said Bat with enthusiasm. 'Boat!'

Bat looked out to the river and contorted his face. 'So...there's a boat out there, is there?'

Bolt and Dealer rolled their eyes in despair.

Onboard the 'OWMUTCH', in the lower cabin, sat

Scott Flowers opposite his old friend Jerry Coe. On a nearby table sat three of Scott's giant henchmen playing cards. It was a luxurious boat, very cosy and homely, and the atmosphere was relaxed and friendly. Scott was looking tired from being up all night, and had been knocking back coffee in abundance trying to perk himself up. Jerry, on the other hand, was buzzing with anticipation:

'Lovely boat, Scotty,' he said, extremely impressed with the surroundings. 'Yours?'

'No, just borrowing it,' explained Scott, knocking back his fourth cup. 'It's perfect for doing business - nice and secluded.'

Jerry smiled. 'Good choice. I have to admit, I was getting a tad worried that you weren't gonna have the money in time,' he said with nervous relief in his voice.

Scott smiled reassuringly and placed a money-bag on the table:

'Don't be stupid Jez, I told you it was as safe as houses,' he said smugly.

'You certainly did. Nice one, Scotty,' said Jerry, and reached for the bag.

Scott placed his hand on top of it:

'Just one thing...,' said Scott.

'What's up?'

'You didn't tell Donald about this, did you?' asked

Scott with concern.

'Of course not,' replied Jerry, brushing it aside as a stupid question.

Deep down Scott believed that Jerry would be true to his word and not let on, but on this occasion he needed reassurance - Donald Kelly was not a man to be messed with:

'Are you sure?' asked Scott, double-checking.

'Fuck's sake Scott, I'm your mate,' replied Jerry breaking into a laugh. 'Believe me, if Donald knew about this, you'd be paying him back twice as much - you know that.'

Scott smiled and gently nodded in agreement – he was reassured and removed his hand from the bag. Jerry grabbed it and opened it excitedly, but his face soon dropped - the bag contained bundles of cut-out pieces of newspaper. Jerry quickly rummaged around inside the bag, pulling out the bundles and searching for the cash, but to his confusion, there wasn't any.

At first Jerry wasn't overly concerned and let out a 'you got me' type laugh, believing he was the victim of one of Scotty's practical jokes, but the atmosphere changed as the henchmen got to their feet.

Jerry smiled nervously. 'This is a joke, right?' he said to his old friend.

Scott's face was serious and unwavering, he slowly shook his head:

'No, it's no joke.'

Jerry's eyes were fixed on Scott's face, looking for telltale signs of a prank, but there weren't any. He glanced over to the henchmen who were standing in a line, looking fiercely at him and blocking any chance of an exit. He turned back to Scott whose expression hadn't altered. Jerry was stunned, his stomach slowly sank, his eyes opened wide with fear and they began to fill. Scott was impassive, there was a coldness in his eyes that Jerry had seen before – in the eyes of Donald Kelly, one of the most ruthless gangsters he had ever known. A lump came to Jerry's throat and he was stripped of speech – the terror on his face alone was pleading with Scott.

From the embankment, Dealer spotted movement on deck:

''ere we go,' he alerted Bolt and Bat, then watched events unfold through the binoculars.

Scott emerged on deck, closely followed by his three henchmen manhandling Jerry, who was by this time absolutely panic-stricken – the reality had set in and his knees had began to buckle from fear. He was held upright and frog-marched towards Scott who produced an eight-inch serrated edged fishing knife. Jerry looked at the blade with dread - a cold shiver ran down his spine. He struggled in vain to free himself from the tight grip of the henchmen:

'Scotty, you don't have to do this!' sobbed Jerry, pleading for his life. 'Keep the money, I won't say anythin', it's not worth my life!'

'Can't do that, Jerry,' said Scott, almost apologetically. 'I gotta finish it now, or I'll be forever lookin' over my shoulder.'

Jerry's stomach sank to new depths, tears streaming - he pleaded again, struggling to get the words out:

'For Christ's sake, Scotty...'

Scott had heard enough - he ruthlessly plunged the knife hard into Jerry's stomach. Time seemed to stand still as Jerry gasped for breath, he slowly dropped to his knees still propped up by the henchmen. Scott mercilessly stabbed him several more times in the chest, until Jerry no longer moved.

The henchmen dragged Jerry's lifeless body to the edge of the boat, then slid it face down gently into the river. As they stood watching the body drift away, Scott did the unthinkable and licked the blood from the knife.

Dealer and Bolt were disturbed by what they had witnessed.

'Did you see that, Bolt?' asked Dealer.

'I saw it,' replied Bolt, in deep shock.

'Bat?' asked Dealer.

Bat was wearing a huge smile:

'Yeah...it's a blue boat, right?'

Dealer and Bolt chose to ignore Bat. A brief moment passed as they tried to absorb what had just happened. Bolt turned to Dealer:

'You knew that was gonna 'appen, didn't ya?'

'I had a hunch,' answered Dealer evasively.

'Fuck, what are we gonna do now?' wondered Bolt.

'I know exactly what to do now,' replied Dealer, who calmly produced his mobile phone. Dealer was up on his feet and heading away. 'Come on,' he called out.

It took a second for Bolt to get going, he was still fixated on the boat, and irritated at Dealer's sudden coolness. He aggressively grabbed hold of Bat by the jacket:

'Come on you,' he said, dragging Bat to his feet.

Dealer walked rapidly along the grass track embankment, with Bolt and Bat close on his heels. Without breaking stride, he produced the 'letter' from within his jacket, opened it out and quickly checked the contents, whilst Bolt watched with curiosity. He then pressed a speed-dial number on his phone:

"ello...Stan, it's Dealer...I need fifty grand's worth of Bool Technology shares right away ...that's the one....yes I'm fuckin' sure....good. I'll call ya later.'

Bolt was bewildered:

'What the fuck was that about?' he asked, clearly irritated.

Bat had veered off course and Bolt dragged him back by the shoulder.

'It's personal,' replied Dealer, hiding the 'letter' and picking up the pace. 'Come on, we gotta weddin' to go to.'

'Oh I love weddings,' said Bat with excitement. 'I went to a pornographic weddin' once, all the bridesmaids were naked and all the pages were stuck together.'

'Oh shut up!' Dealer and Bolt snapped in unison.

12:40PM

A line of ten white stretch Limousines, adorned with white ribbons, were parked outside St Mary the Virgin – a beautiful 14th century parish church located in the heart of Buntleyford village. Dealer's Range Rover pulled up sharply nearby, and Dealer, Bolt and Bat exited in a hurry. They could hear the sound of church bells ringing out, and Dealer was anxious that he might be too late.

Inside the church, the Minister - attired in a long white cassock, was midway through the marriage service. The pews were jam-packed with people, and Sally was looking radiant in her stunning white bridal gown as she stood alongside her beloved husband-to-be, Quinton - himself looking handsome in a dazzling white, tailor-made, three piece suit.

It was a motley gathering - the two sides of the congregation reflecting the two families, and they couldn't be more different: On one side of the church sat monstrously huge gangsters all dressed in black, looking as hard as nails – wearing gold chains and diamond encrusted rings, bracelets and watches. Their identikit Barbie doll wives and girlfriends at their sides – chewing gum and completely OTT with their apparel; fur coats, short skirts, fishnet stockings, bursting cleavages, wall-to-wall bling and multi-layered make-up - so heavily piled on that they wouldn't dare raise an eyebrow for fear of cracking the foundation on their chins. Half the planet's peroxide had gone into these ladies and they were constantly checking their vanity mirrors for a hair that might be out of place; for the majority of these women, it was the perfect opportunity to flaunt themselves. Amongst the gangster congregation sat Vanessa with her giant seven-foot gangster husband. Vanessa was in tears, her nose running, overcome with the emotion of the occasion:

'They're so perfect for each other,' she sobbed. 'Match made in 'eaven.'

She reached over and removed a white handkerchief from the top pocket of her husband's jacket, and blew her nose hard into it, whilst her husband looked at her and grimaced in disgust.

In total contrast, filling the other side of the congregation, were very ordinary (noticeably poorer) Italian peasant folk – family that Quinton had flown over from a small Italian fishing town that was at least 40 years behind the times. The men didn't own a smart suit between them; white shirts, old trousers and non-matching waistcoats were as much as the majority could muster up, only a handful were wearing neckties, many wore old flat caps. The Minister secretly thought that they looked like a convention for the 'Zorba The Greek' appreciation society – regardless of the fact that they were Italian. The women were attired in their old favourite - mostly hand-me-downs - summer dresses with clashing headscarves, and not a drop of make-up in sight. These were poor simple people, and the dental-work told its own story, as most of the elderly had little to no teeth, but were not ashamed to show their gummy smiles to everyone. As dishevelled as they all looked, they were humble folk, salt of the earth, and extremely grateful and happy to be there.

Maria Verani sat on the front pew of the Italian congregation, her eyes streaming. She felt a tap on the shoulder and turned to look. It was an old, toothless, Italian friend of the family:

'You musta' be ver' happiness',' he said to Maria, in a barely understandable pidgin English, a phrase he had learnt on the plane flying over.

Maria was anything but happy:

'My son 'ees wanker!' she exclaimed, and burst out crying into a tissue as she turned back around.

'Ahhh, wanker, wanker,' the old man gleamed

with joy, clearly not understanding, and patting Maria on the shoulder in congratulation.

Meanwhile, outside: Dealer, with a cigar between his teeth, had reached the consecrated inner grounds and was marching swiftly along a narrow footpath that ran parallel to the church, with Bolt and Bat trailing closely. As Dealer turned in sharply towards the main doors, Bat also turned, in the opposite direction, and was rapidly heading away from the church. He skidded to an abrupt halt when Bolt grabbed him by the shoulder and dragged him back behind Dealer and up to the entrance.

Inside the church, the giant oak doors were suddenly thrown open and sent crashing against the walls – *BANG!!* - booming out like a field artillery cannon. The gangster congregation calmly looked over their shoulders to see what the commotion was, while the elderly Italian guests instinctively dived for cover – the noise stirring memories of the horrendous bombing they had endured during World War II. As the resonance began to die out, the startled Italian guests tentatively began to rise, gazing over the pews towards the main doors where they saw the impressive figure of The Dealer standing at the doorway silhouetted against the glaring sunlight directly behind him. Maria crossed herself in awestruck wonder:

'Beelzebub...Prince of Darkness...Sperm of Satan,'

she said to herself with a tremor, and was strangely overcome with sense of optimism.

Sally briefly peered over her shoulder and sighed with relief to see her brother. She had been concerned that he would miss her entire wedding, but now her big day was finally complete and she had never been happier. She turned to Quinton and smiled coyly.

Dealer threw the cigar from his mouth onto the ground outside, then stomped up the aisle with urgency and purpose. Bolt and Bat followed. Whispers of 'Dealer' could be heard as all eyes followed his path towards the pulpit.

The Minister was used to the annoying sound of the outer doors crashing in the wind, and casually continued the service:

'Will you, Sally Dempsey, take this man, Quinton Alessandro Santino Baldovino Verani, to be your lawful wedded husband?'

Sally looked across at Quinton, there was no doubt in her mind. 'I will,' she answered.

Dealer suddenly grabbed Sally's hand:

'Not! You're comin' with me,' he said, pulling her away.

There was a stunned silence - the congregation sat, mouths agape, as Dealer put a halt to the wedding.

'Danny! What are you doing?!!' cried Sally, as Dealer forcibly dragged her back down the aisle.

The Minister and Quinton stood side by side looking on in shock, whilst Bolt watched in confusion.

'I'm savin' my little sister from that two-faced, womanisin', wife beatin', greasy, Italian slimeshit!' growled Dealer as he tightened his grip around Sally.

'Wife beating?!!' yelled Sally in bewilderment. 'What are you talking about, we're not even married yet!! Let go!!' she cried, desperately trying to cling onto a pew.

'Come on!!' insisted Dealer, easily overpowering her, and continued dragging her down the aisle and out of the church.

Over at the giant pipe organ, sat the village organist wearing a broad grin, his warped sense of humour had got the better of him and, in an ironic fashion, began playing the hymn 'All Things Bright And Beautiful'. He beckoned over to the smirking choir, who simultaneously began to sing along.

Bat was in gangster mode - with sheer aggression he stormed over to the pulpit and grabbed hold of who he believed to be Quinton.

'You heard, slimeshit!' snarled Bat, like a deranged dingo. 'You get yer hands off The Dealer's sister, or I'll kick ya between the legs so hard, you'll 'ave three Adam's apples!'

'BAT!!' cried Bolt in horror – realising that Bat had mistakenly grabbed and confronted the Minister.

Quinton was standing alongside watching numbly.

Bolt dragged Bat away by the collar.

'Sorry about that, Mister Minister, it's his eyes,' explained Bolt.

The Minister calmly adjusted his ruffled cassock:

'Ahh yes...,' he said to himself, 'the old *"eyes, balls and throat"* routine.'

He looked over to a stunned Quinton, who was standing with his mouth open.

'...And how was your holiday?' the Minister enquired.

Bolt was escorting Bat back down the aisle:

'Minister?' said Bat in horror. 'Did you say Minister? Fuck! What did I just say?'

'Put it this way; I'd give the church fete a miss next year,' explained Bolt.

The congregation were still completely stupefied - all that is, except Maria; her hands were clasped together in prayer. She looked up to heavens with elation, and mouthed the words *'Thank you'*.

The overzealous organist was in full swing as the choir joyously sang out, with one obese choirboy - in true gospel fashion - adlibbing wildly over the top.

The Minister looked sharply at the organist:

'Do you mind?!!' he shouted sternly.

The organist came to an abrupt halt, and the choir quickly followed.

'Thank you!' said the Minister, then whispered the word 'Tosser' under his breath as he turned to face Quinton.

Quinton was motionless, still numb with shock, his eyes fixed on the main doors where he had last seen his beloved. The Minister waved a hand in front of Quinton's face and clicked his fingers several times - there was no reaction.

'Houston, we have a problem,' said the Minister.

Quinton held the stunned expression as he slowly fell forward and crashed to the wooden floor - *THUD!* - out cold.

Gangster wife Vanessa, wiped her nose into her husband's handkerchief:

'Told ya it would never fuckin' work,' she said nonchalantly, and stuffed the soiled handkerchief back into her husband's top pocket.

12:47PM

Dealer had dragged his sister back to the Range Rover in the church's car park, and forced her onto the rear seat alongside Bolt. Bat had made his way to the passenger seat, whilst Dealer climbed into the driver's seat and slammed the door shut. Sally was livid and in floods of tears:

'I hate you! I hate you!!!' she screamed hysterically at her brother, with Bolt flinching at every sentence. 'How can you do this to me?!!!'

'Quinton is scum,' said Dealer bluntly. 'He'll lie, he'll cheat, he'll make yer life fuckin' hell!' he yelled back at her.

Sally was bemused: 'But yesterday, you thought the world of him!!'

'That was yesterday!' snapped Dealer. 'Today I know better. You'll thank me for this later.'

'Thank you?!!' screamed Sally in disbelief. 'Oh thank you, Danny. Thank you so much,' she sarcastically continued. 'Thank you for ruining the best day of my fucking life!!'

'Watch yer mouth!' demanded Dealer.

'Or what?! What are you gonna do, Danny?! Put me over your knee and spank me?!!'

'Oh. Can I watch, Dan?' interrupted Bat jokingly.

'Shut it, Bat!' replied Dealer, and started the engine.

Moments later they were speeding away from the church along a picturesque country lane, with Sally still seeing red:

'I'm not a child anymore, damn it!! I'm a grown woman!!!' she blasted at the top of her voice.

'I don't care 'ow old you are! I'm always gonna be yer big brother!' yelled Dealer back at her. 'And if I say ya don't marry, ya don't fuckin' marry! Got it?!!'

Hysteria set in. 'Then I'll kill myself!!' screamed Sally opening the rear door in an attempt to throw herself from the moving vehicle.

'Shit!' panicked Bolt, who quickly grabbed onto her as she hung out of the car.

The Range Rover swerved from one side of the road to the other as Dealer tried to control it. Bolt was trying to close the door with one hand whilst desperately clinging on to Sally with the other.

'Let me go! I wanna die!!' she screamed.

'Jesus Christ! Pull her in!' shouted Dealer in a panic.

'I'm pullin', I'm pullin'!!' replied Bolt using every ounce of strength to hang on to her.

The car skidded violently, but Dealer managed to control it, and pulled it over safely to the side of the road. He let out a huge sigh of relief.

Bolt pulled Sally back into the car, she was crying uncontrollably. Dealer listened to her wail for a minute, before finally beginning to feel some sympathy. He exited the car and tentatively got into the rear seat next to her.

'Look, Sal...,' said Dealer, reaching out to put a comforting arm around her.

'Don't touch me! Just don't touch me!!' snapped Sally.

'Okay, okay. I won't touch ya,' said Dealer, backing away.

'Can I touch her?' joked Bat.

'Will you shut the fuck up, Bat?!' growled Dealer.

'I'm shut, I'm shut.' assured Bat – his silence only lasting a moment. 'Do you want me to drive now, Dealer?'

'NO!!' came the panicked reply, blasted in unison by Dealer, Bolt and Sally.

Dealer had had enough of Bat:

'Tell ya what, Bat, why don't ya go for a walk, go on! And get me a fuckin' paper!'

'No probs,' said Bat opening the door. 'I think we

passed some shops back there.'

Bat exited the car and turned in all directions trying to get his bearings:

'Shops, shops, shops.....,' he muttered, scrunching his eyes and scratching his head. 'This way I reckon,' he said with confidence, and headed off - convinced he knew where he was going.

Bolt watched as Bat wandered into no man's land – a large open field with nothing in the distant horizon but a few trees.

'Oh for fuck's sake!' said Bolt, totally pissed off. 'BAT!!' he yelled, then leapt from the car to go and rescue him.

Sally was still weeping.

'Look, Sal,' said Dealer gently, trying to console his sister. 'I know it looks as though I may 'ave fucked things up for ya....'

'MAY HAVE?!!' erupted Sally.

'But I swear on mum and dad's grave that by tonight, I'd 'ave made it up to ya - big time,' assured Dealer.

Sally suddenly calmed, and seemed strangely in control of her emotions:

'Really, Danny?' she asked, wiping away her tears.

'Promise,' replied Dealer soothingly.

'Tonight?' asked Sally, sniffling her running nose.

Dealer smiled reassuringly:

'Tonight,' he confirmed.

'Okay...,' said Sally checking the clock on the dash board, '...well, that gives me about eight hours.... to FUCKING HATE YOU!!!'

Sally suddenly exploded, unleashing a barrage of vicious and uncontrolled punches and slaps:

'I HATE YOU!!! I HATE YOU!!!' she screamed, as she laid into her brother.

Dealer huddled up into a ball. 'OW..Fuck...stop it, you nut! Get off!!'

The onslaught continued. 'I'LL KILL YOU, YOU BASTARD!!'

Meanwhile, Bolt had retrieved Bat, and they were heading back towards the car when Bolt suddenly stopped: He could see the Range Rover just up ahead rocking to the muffled sound of Sally and Dealer's groans. Bat stopped alongside Bolt and looked on in astonishment.

'Well, would you believe it...,' said Bat, 'his own sister.....dirty bastard.'

Bolt looked at Bat in bewilderment.

1:15PM

Professor Pringle was inside a very busy London branch of the 'TWB' bank, being led through a crowd of customers to an interview room.

'Just go on in,' said the female bank clerk politely with a smile, leaving him to it.

Pringle was a jittery bundle of nerves. He knocked and tentatively opened the door to be greeted by the bank manager, Mr Andrew Swift, who quickly rose and smiled warmly.

'Mr Prongle,' said Swift, offering his hand from across a desk.

'Are you really?' said Pringle, pleasantly surprised. 'How extraordinary. I'm Pringle,' he explained and shook hands with zeal. 'Fancy that; Prongle and Pringle.'

Swift was perplexed. 'No,' he explained, pointing to the nametag pinned to his lapel, his name '*Manager - Mr Andrew Swift*' clearly embossed in gold letters. 'I'm Swift.'

'Glad to hear it,' said Pringle, ignoring the tag, 'I

have rather a lot on today myself.'

Swift was baffled but felt it probably best to move on with the interview. 'Umm... Won't you sit down?' he offered.

'Yes, thank you.'

Swift opened out an application form:

'I've been looking over your loan application.'

'Ahh yes,' said Pringle, suddenly remembering why he was there. He crossed his legs and - *WHACK!* - accidentally kicked a pen rack that was slightly overhanging the desk. The pens flew everywhere.

'Oh, I'm so sorry,' apologised Pringle in a panic. 'How clumsy of me,' and was quickly down on his knees trying to pick them all up.

'That's okay,' said Swift, seemingly unfazed. 'Please don't worry, Mr Pringle, I'll sort that out.'

'Are you sure?' asked Pringle, popping his head up from behind the desk.

'Yes, quite sure,' assured Swift. 'Please sit down.'

'Okay,' said Pringle, sitting himself back down with the handful of pens he had gathered. 'How embarrassing,' he fumbled.

He placed the pens onto the desk, then watched them slowly roll back onto the floor. Pringle forced a smile.

Swift elected to ignore the incident:

'Now..., I see you work for the *Strumwick Scientific*

Research Laboratories,' he said, referring to the application.

'Sorry, it must be my writing; that should read *Strudwick*...' explained Pringle, leaning forward to point at his mistake on the form. '...Only I don't work there anymore.'

At that moment, Pringle's coat sleeve caught a steaming hot cup of coffee, which spilt onto the desk and ran straight into Swift's lap. Swift was up like a shot:

'ARGHHH!'

'Oh my goodness!' said Pringle in a panic. 'I'm so sorry.'

While Swift was frantically shaking the excess coffee from his trousers, Pringle got to his feet, anxious to help:

'Here, let me mop you down,' he said in a fluster.

'No, no, it's nothing,' said Swift, determined to keep Pringle at arm's length.

'Are you sure? I've got a handkerchief...' explained Pringle, who rummaged through his coat pockets and bizarrely produced a tin of cat food.

'I'm fine! Please sit down,' insisted Swift, who was beginning to lose patience.

'Oh,' said Pringle, abashed by Swift's bluntness. 'Okay.'

He put the tin back inside his coat and re-seated

himself.

Swift picked up the coffee-drenched application form, and shook it vigorously:

'You say you don't work at *Strudwick* anymore?' he asked, with an edge to his voice.

'No, I had a slight....accident,' explained Pringle tentatively.

'Hmmm........,' said Swift with suspicion.

Pringle suddenly felt uncomfortable, and became fidgety. He picked up a large elastic band from the table and stretched it out between his thumbs.

Swift had seen and heard enough:

'I won't beat about the bush, Mr Pringle.'

'Oh please don't, Mr Prongle.'

The outstretched elastic band flew out of Pringle's hand and – *WHACK!* - Swift got it straight in the eye:

'ARGHHHH!' he yelled, and keeled over in agony.

Pringle looked on in horror:

'Whoops,' he said timidly.

Moments later, Pringle was being politely escorted out of the bank by two members of staff. He was guilt-ridden and extremely embarrassed:

'I'm so sorry,' he said, 'I do hope Prongle's eye will be okay.'

The staff left Pringle on the footpath outside the door, and turned back inside with a sense of relief.

Pringle let out a despondent sigh. He produced a small notebook and opened it up to view a long list of high street banks – of which the first three had already been crossed off. He then put a line through the fourth – 'TWB BANK'.

2:26PM

Donald Kelly was seated between The Twins in the rear of his black Limousine as it travelled at speed along a country lane. Behind their dark glasses, The Twins' eyes were fixed on Scott Flowers, who sat facing them in the rear compartment. Donald had both hands firmly on the black executive briefcase resting securely on his lap. He looked apprehensive. Under normal circumstances Scott would be laying bricks in the presence of Donald and his henchmen; Scott was under no illusions, he knew that Donald disliked him immensely but this was business, and Scott was confident - to the point of being cocky - that Donald would be grateful for the deal he had set up for the paintings.

Mickey was driving - steering with one hand whilst holding a mobile phone to his ear with the other. He was somewhat frustrated:

'I dunno where Jerry is, boss,' he said, tossing his phone onto the passenger seat. 'He's not at home, not at the office, and his mobile keeps goin' to voicemail.'

'Well, did you leave him a message?' asked Donald.

Mickey was thrown off-guard by the question. 'Oh...no. Sorry boss, did ya want me to?'

'That would be nice, Mickey, thank you,' replied Donald condescendingly.

The mention of Jerry made Scott uncomfortable, he purposely slipped his dark glasses on – an old gambler's trick used in poker to avoid giving anything away with eye movement; he was aware that Donald was a master at poker, and at reading people's faces. It crossed Scott's mind that putting the glasses on at that precise moment may make Donald suspicious, but fortunately for him, Donald didn't clock it and Scott quickly changed the subject to divert his attention:

'We're nearly there, Don,' said Scott peering out of the window - words that put Donald on edge.

In a nearby country pub, Dealer, Bolt, Bat and Sally were seated at a table with their backs to a large frosted window, pints of lager in front of them. While the three men were happily knocking back their drinks, Sally - still distraught, and in her wedding dress - stared aimlessly into space, her pint untouched. Dealer was studying the racing page of a newspaper opened out in front of him and was jotting down his horse selection.

Sally let out a heavy sigh:

'Ohhhh, Mumm Mummm Mumm Mummm Mumm,' she softly mumbled – her sighs being completely ignored.

'Since when do you do the horses, Dealer?' enquired Bolt.

'Since today,' replied Dealer - who produced the 'letter' to check its contents.

Bolt watched with curiosity:

'What is that letter?' he asked as he tried to take a sneaky look.

Dealer snatched it from sight. 'Personal, I told ya!' he said sternly.

'I used to go to the horses all the time,' remarked Bat, in passing.

Bolt had to think hard. 'No you didn't,' he said argumentatively.

'Fuckin' did,' insisted Bat.

'Where at?' asked Bolt.

'Catford!' snapped Bat.

'They were dogs, you clown!'

'Same difference,' said Bat smugly.

Sally let out another despairing sigh:

'Ohhh, Quin Quin Quin Quin Quin,' she softly mumbled – again her sighs completely ignored.

Dealer put the 'letter' away and returned to writing his horse selection, when he suddenly remembered:

'Shit! What's the time, Bolt?'

Bolt tutted. 'Nearly half past,' he replied abruptly, resenting the fact that Dealer was constantly using him as his timepiece.

'I better get ready,' said Dealer reaching inside his pocket.

Donald's Limo pulled up sharply outside the pub. The Twins emerged first, checking for any sign of potential trouble. When they were completely satisfied that the coast was clear, they held the rear doors open. Donald and Scott made a hasty exit.

Donald put on a dark pair of shades as Scott led the way to the pub's entrance, with The Twins and Mickey trailing closely. As they drew near, Donald hesitated:

'Is this it?' he asked apprehensively.

'Yeah,' replied Scott. 'What's up, Don, ya don't look that happy?'

'This ain't my patch, Scott, I'm never happy when I'm not on my own turf,' explained Donald. 'And this 'Dealer' geezer - I've heard some disturbin' shit about him.'

'Donald, how many times? He's as safe as houses,' explained Scott with a blasé attitude that wound Donald up no end.

'I've heard he's a fuckin' lunatic!' growled Donald, leaning into Scott.

'Was, Don, was,' quickly assured Scott, trying to calm the situation. 'Look, all them stories you hear about Dealer are things he done back in his twenties - a long time ago. Nowadays Dealer's mellowed, he's highly respected.'

Donald was still not entirely convinced, his doubts not helped by the fact that he despised Scott and couldn't shake off a niggling feeling that Scott was not to be trusted. Donald held up the briefcase:

'There's a lot at stake here,' he said menacingly.

Scott acknowledged by gently nodding.

'Dealer's a sound businessman - with incredible connections,' assured Scott, and strolled to the entrance. 'Just come in and meet him. He's just a normal bloke that hangs around with normal people, everything's normal and he trusts me implicitly.'

Scott swung the pub door open and held it as an invitation for Donald to enter. Donald took a brief moment to consider:

'You better be fuckin' right, Scott,' he threatened, as he headed through the door.

'Safe as houses,' said Scott smugly, and followed Donald in, with Mickey and The Twins on his heels.

They had barely taken a few steps inside when all five stopped dead in their tracks - a look of disbelief on Donald and Scott's faces. Dealer was seated facing them wearing a mocking grin and a lit cigar between his teeth, on his head was a multicoloured Beanie cap with revolving propeller - whirling around to a high pitched buzz. Seated on Dealer's left was Bat, with his thick lens glasses, tapping the ash out of his cigarette into his own half full pint glass. To Dealer's right sat Sally, in her bridal gown, tears rolling down her cheeks, staring despairingly into space. Her mascara-smudged panda eyes slowly turned towards Donald:

'Help me. Please, help me,' she softly pleaded.

Bat took a swig of his beer and instantly spat it out:

'Beer's off!' he said, cringing from the cigarette ash lodged in his throat.

Both Donald and Scott simultaneously lifted their shades up over their eyes to double-check that what they were seeing was for real. Donald turned to Scott with a face of thunder. Scott was dumbstruck - quaking in his shoes, he foolishly let out an uncontrolled nervous laugh. Big mistake - Donald erupted:

'Out of my fuckin' way!!' he blasted, as he about-turned and stormed out, knocking aside Mickey and The Twins en route.

Scott slowly shuffled towards Dealer:

'What the fuck are you doing, Dealer?' he said, stricken with panic. 'He's gonna fuckin' kill me!!'

'You lucky thing,' said Sally numbly.

Bat suddenly perked up, he recognised Scott's

voice and was pleasantly surprised:

'Scotty? 'ow the fuck are ya?' he said with a broad grin, and stood up to offer his hand - pointing it completely in the wrong direction.

Dealer removed the comical cap and got to his feet. His smile turned to anger as he leant into Scott's face.

'No more than you deserve, you back stabbin' piece of shit!' growled Dealer through gritted teeth. 'Or maybe I should say – chest stabbin'.'

Scott froze in horror, the hairs on the back of his neck standing on end, wondering how much Dealer actually knew, or how it could be possible that Dealer knew anything at all. But it was too much of a coincidence, it had only been the day before that he and Dealer were the closest of friends - for Dealer to turn like this could only mean that word was out. Scott looked Dealer in the eyes, Dealer's face was unwavering - awash with hatred. Scott was petrified, his stomach began to churn. He glanced over his shoulder to see that Mickey and The Twins were waiting for him at the exit. He looked back at Dealer – it was do or die time for Scott. He suddenly raced towards a side window and launched himself through the glass - *CRASH!* - shattering it into pieces. He hit the pavement hard, blood dripping from glass splinter wounds to his face and hands. He staggered to his feet; he had fallen awkwardly and held his left leg in considerable pain as he desperately limped away.

Upon hearing the smash, Mickey and The Twins rushed into the pub and over to the shattered window.

'Oh shit,' said Mickey, poking his head through the broken glass - there was no sign of Scott, the street was deserted. He turned back inside:

'Come on!' he said urgently to The Twins, and led them in pursuit of Scott through the main doors.

Bolt had been watching events from the bar, and calmly returned to the table brandishing a fresh pint of lager.

Bat seated himself back down and suddenly felt a chill across his back. He looked around:

'Somebody shut the window!' he yelled. 'Bloody freezin' in 'ere.'

Dealer and Bolt ignored him.

'Serves Scott right,' said Bolt turning to Dealer. 'Shame about Donald though, I reckon you could 'ave done some serious business with him.'

'You reckon?' said Dealer nonchalantly. 'I reckon he'll be behind bars by Thursday.'

'Yeah?' said Bolt, baffled. 'What makes you so sure?'

'Never mind,' said Dealer. 'Drink up, I need ya to get down the bookies.'

Dealer passed his betting selection over to Bolt, who looked at it with suspicion as he started to down his pint.

Donald had stormed back to the Limousine. His mind was working ten to the dozen, scheming all the things he was going to do to Scott when he laid his hands on him. The Limo doors opened, and Mickey and The Twins climbed in.

'Well, where is he?!' blasted Donald.

'Sorry boss,' replied Mickey timidly, 'we lost him.'

'You fuckin' idiots!!' erupted Donald, causing Mickey to flinch.

Mickey turned to The Twins:

'Idiots!!' he shouted, displacing the blame.

The Twins turned to each other and shrugged their shoulders, unaffected by Mickey's slur.

'I want him found, and I want him fuckin' brought to me! Do you understand?!!' continued Donald, directly at Mickey.

Mickey again turned to The Twins:

'Well, do you?!!' he yelled.

The Twins looked down their noses at Mickey:

'Yeah, we understand,' they both answered, in a belittling manner.

Mickey turned back to Donald:

'They understand, boss,' he said reassuringly.

Donald was increasingly vexed with Mickey's smart-arse attitude. He gritted his teeth ready lay into him, but Mickey quickly jumped in:

'Look, don't worry, boss.' he said with a hand held out in placation. 'We'll put the word out. We'll get him.'

2:48PM

Scott was sweating, out of breath and exhausted. He had run as far as he could with the excruciating pain in his injured leg and had slowed down to a near standstill. He produced his mobile phone and limped to the nearest tree to take cover. He was terrified, the phone was shaking in his hand as he scrolled through '*contacts*' to find his brother Jeff.

Jeff was at home in the kitchen going through his bills and bank statements. He was faced with the daunting task of having to reshuffle all of his finances to account for the money that his wife had lent to Scott – money that would have covered their monthly mortgage repayment. From past experience Jeff knew that Scott wouldn't be forthcoming in repaying his debts, so he couldn't rely on ever seeing the money again – which left a bitter taste in his mouth; he feared that his family would struggle in the months ahead.

His wife Anne was in the background, quietly preparing a meal. She was riddled with guilt for putting her family in this position, and was conscious not to make any noise or interfere while Jeff tried to figure things out – she felt that she had done enough damage.

As Jeff slumped back into his seat feeling defeated with the figures, the house phone rang. He sluggishly made his way to the hall and picked up the handset:

'Hello,' he said dispiritedly.

'Jeff, it's me, Scott.'

Jeff was stunned, he couldn't believe that Scott would have the audacity to call.

'Jeff, you gotta help me, bruv,' continued Scott in desperation. 'I'm in big trouble.'

'You've got a fuckin' nerve, after what you did to Anne,' said Jeff, outraged.

Anne had overheard and strolled into the hallway.

'It's nothin' to do with money this time. I've got all the money in the world,' said Scott - for once telling the truth. And, at that precise moment, he really didn't care about his 'blood money'.

'You're so full of shit,' said Jeff.

'No, I swear,' pleaded Scott. 'I can pay you back double...triple! I just need a place to stay! Can you come and get me?'

'You are un-fuckin'-believable!' said Jeff. He looked over to Anne, pointed at the handset, and laughed mockingly.

'Please Jeff,' said Scott in a panic, 'I'm desperate!

It's life or death.'

Jeff still didn't believe his brother, he shrugged his shoulders:

'Then I choose death,' he said without feeling.

'You don't understand...' Scott tried to explain, but Jeff had heard enough and turned angry:

'Listen carefully, Scott, I don't care that you're my brother, the next time I see you, I'm gonna fuckin' lay you out for what you did to Anne!'

'But bruv...,' cried Scott.

'Now fuckin' stay away from me and my family!!' threatened Jeff, and with that, slammed the phone down.

'Jeff! Jeff!...,' called Scott in desperation. The phone was dead. 'Fuck it!' he shouted.

He slumped against the tree and looked to the Heavens, desperately trying to think where he could go, or who he could call. He quickly decided that he couldn't afford to be seen out in the open. He checked that the coast was clear around him, then, with what little energy he had left, cautiously limped away.

3:00PM

Dealer pulled his Range Rover up outside Buntleyford Town Hall. He quickly applied the handbrake and turned off the engine. Sally, in her wedding dress - still tearful and devastated, was sitting lifelessly in the rear seat next to Bat, pining for her Quinton. Bolt was in the passenger seat looking perturbed, he turned to Dealer:

'What are we stoppin' 'ere for?' he asked.

'I figured now is as good a time as any to 'ave a word with my friendly local Councillor,' replied Dealer.

'Councillor Plummer?' wondered Bolt.

'Yep,' said Dealer opening the door.

'What about?' asked Bolt, still bemused.

'Him givin' me some government storage space,' answered Dealer coolly.

'You can't be serious,' said Bolt. 'He fuckin' hates you!'

'So?' said Dealer undisturbed, as he stepped out from the car.

Bolt was not at all happy, but quickly followed. Dealer poked his head back inside:

'Bat, stay 'ere with Sally. Don't let her out' the car.'

'Right, got ya,' said Bat enthusiastically and acknowledged the command by crassly sticking his thumbs up.

Dealer and Bolt slammed their doors shut and hastily headed off towards the Town Hall entrance. Sally was lost in a world of her own, staring aimlessly out of the window.

'What's it all about, Bat?' she asked despondently.

Bat didn't have a clue what was going on at the best of times, and he certainly hadn't a clue what Sally was asking, but felt obliged to answer:

'Well...Dealer's gonna ask a plumber to give him some counsellin'...,' he fumbled, trying to figure things out in his own head as he spoke. 'And...'

'What did I do to deserve this?' interrupted Sally numbly, paying no attention to Bat. 'Was I pure evil in my previous life?' she wondered.

'Possibly...,' explained Bat, '... a mass murderer, or one of those 'she devils' - what do they call 'em? 'Lady Boys'. I don't think I was even born in my previous life.'

Again Sally wasn't listening to Bat's nonsensical drivel. She let out a sigh:

'What's Quinton doing now?' she pondered,

heartbroken.

Bat mulled over the possibilities:

'Could be doing anythin'...drugs, watchin' telly, ...drinkin' soup... havin' a dump...'

'Is he hurting inside as much as me?' she wondered, still oblivious to Bat's existence.

Bat was stumped by the question. He scratched his head:

'...Depends if he's constipated,' he surmised.

Sally let out another sigh:

'Ohhh.'

Quinton was lying on his bed still fully dressed in his wedding suit. He too was devastated, and stared aimlessly at the ceiling.

'Ohhh,' he sighed.

His mother Maria tentatively entered the room carrying a bowl of soup. What she thought was going to be the worst day of her life, had miraculously turned in her favour, and her only child was back home - exactly where she wanted him.

'Quinton, I make'a you some nice hot soup,' said Maria as she slowly approached. 'You like'a your Mamma's soup...put some hairs on your bollocks.'

Quinton let out another sigh:

'Ohhh.'

'Whadd'a matter, Quinton?' asked Maria with

sympathy. 'Talk'a to your Mamma,' she said, pleading with her son.

'What happened, Mamma?' wondered Quinton. 'One minute I was the happiest man in the world, about to be married - the next...I'm pubic enemy number one.'

'Quinton, my son, 'ow can I say dis without 'urting your feelings?' answered Maria with the utmost affection. 'Drink'a your soup and forget dat slut bitch, she's nuttin' but'a trouble.'

Quinton slowly sat up and looked at the soup, he was too cut up to even think about nourishment, all he wanted to do was crawl into a hole and die.

'No thanks, Mamma,' he said in a daze, 'I need something stronger.'

Maria took a sharp intake of breath:

'You donn'a like'a your Mamma's soup?!!' she said, mortified at the suggestion.

WHACK! - Maria clouted Quinton hard across the head, sending him flying off the bed and onto the floor.

3:06PM

Without a prior appointment, Dealer and Bolt had managed to blag their way in to see Councillor Plummer, and were seated opposite him across a desk in his office at the Town Hall. Dealer was sitting smugly, cross-legged and smoking a cigar, cool and confident, whilst Bolt sat open mouthed. Plummer looked at Dealer with contempt, he couldn't believe what he was hearing:

'Let's make sure I fully understand what you're asking, Mister Dempsey...' said Plummer, who smiled mockingly.

Dealer returned the same mocking smile:

'Let's,' he said.

'Yeah, let's,' agreed Bolt to Dealer, still gobsmacked from the first time he had heard it.

'You want me to supply you with a Government building...' said Plummer.

'With 24-hour surveillance,' said Dealer jumping in, and pointing his cigar to emphasise the point.

'...With surveillance,' corrected Plummer. 'Then

return all your... 'imported goods', so that you can store them under government protection?'

Bolt was still gaping - he had heard correctly the first time, but still couldn't believe his ears.

'...And in return,' continued Plummer, 'you'll give me a handsome little 'backhander' each month?'

'You've got it,' said Dealer contentedly.

Bolt buried his head in his hands. A few seconds passed as the Councillor began to burn up inside with rage, then he let rip:

'Who the fuck do you think I am?!' he exploded. 'Do you think I'm one of your cheap hoods that will bend over backwards to kiss your backside?!'

'Neat trick, if you can do it, Councillor,' said Dealer calmly.

'This may come as a shock to you, Dempsey, but I don't like you,' said Plummer through gritted teeth. 'I hate you, and everything you fucking stand for. 'Far as I'm concerned you are the scum of the Earth that needs to be behind bars!'

Bolt was dumbfounded. He looked at the Councillor who was bright red in the face - about to blow a fuse, then he looked over to Dealer who was completely unfazed. Bolt recollected that only a short while ago Dealer had said that Plummer was a very dangerous man, and now here he was antagonising the shit out of him. Something was amiss, and Bolt stared sceptically at Dealer.

Plummer was up on his feet:

'Now you've got exactly ten seconds to get out of my office, or I will call the police and file charges of attempting to bribe a government Minister!' he yelled.

Bolt was up, extremely worried:

'Come on, Dealer, let's get the fuck out of 'ere.'

Dealer was still calm and collected. He sat firm.

'Two words for ya, Councillor...' said Dealer.

Plummer and Bolt froze in anticipation of the words. But Dealer screwed his face up trying to think – he had forgotten them.

'Fuck. 'old on,' said Dealer reaching inside his jacket pocket, 'I've got 'em written down.'

Plummer picked up the handset of the office phone:

'Five seconds,' he said, with finger poised on the keypad.

Bolt was panicking:

'Dealer, let's go!' he urged.

Dealer calmly produced the 'letter', opened it out and quickly began to scan, whilst Bolt watched with growing unease.

'Oh yeah...' remembered Dealer, then counted the words on his fingers as he read them out. 'Edmund - fuckin' - Woodstock.'

Dealer was holding up three fingers - which confused him as there should have been only two.

Bolt hadn't a clue what was going on, or who Edmund Woodstock was, but he looked over to Councillor Plummer and sensed that Dealer may have touched a nerve.

Plummer was frozen with fear:

'Never heard of him,' he said unconvincingly.

Dealer smiled and placed the cigar between his teeth:

'Well, that's just too fuckin' bad then,' he patronised, then got to his feet and headed for the door. 'Come on, Bolt.'

'Wait!' shouted Plummer in a panic.

That one word was all Bolt needed to hear to know that Dealer had got Plummer by the short and curlies. Dealer and Bolt turned back.

Plummer replaced the handset and slowly sat down, sick with worry – the tables had suddenly turned. Dealer smiled.

Moments later Dealer and Bolt had left Councillor Plummer's office and were rapidly walking through the Town Hall corridor back towards the car. Bolt was annoyed that he was being kept in the dark:

'Who the fuck is Edmund Woodstock?!' he asked.

Dealer shrugged his shoulders:

'A bent MP, his illegitimate son, a gay lover...'

'You mean - ya don't know?!' said Bolt, annoyed.

'Don't know and don't fuckin' care,' replied Dealer. 'Plummer knows *exactly* who he is – and that's all that matters.'

'Why?'

''cause I get my warehouse,' said Dealer smugly.

'You know, you're beginning to scare me, Dealer. What the fuck is going on?! What is that letter? Who is it from?!'

Dealer stopped walking and turned to face Bolt:

'Bolt, do ya mind? I'm fuckin' starvin' - I hate arguin' on an empty stomach.'

Dealer resumed walking:

'Besides,' he continued, talking over his shoulder at Bolt who had remained stationary in a form of protest. 'I've gotta suicidal sister downstairs that I've left alone with Stevie fuckin' Wonder.'

Bolt was peeved, but after a moment of shaking his head in frustration, he quickly caught up with Dealer.

3:15PM

The Minister opened the front door to the vicarage and was startled by the sight of Scott Flowers looking battle-scarred and extremely frightened, blood seeping from wounds to his face that had dripped onto his clothing.

'Sorry to trouble you, Reverend,' said Scott, with a tremor in his voice.

'My God,' said the Minister, '...the Avon Lady.' He opened the door wide for Scott to enter. 'I suppose you'd better come in.'

As Scott hobbled inside, the Minister suddenly panicked as he remembered:

'Please try not to die on the carpet, it's brand new,' he explained, then led the way to an ageing and well worn settee. 'Here, die on this old couch - it's on castors you see...' demonstrating its manoeuvrability by wheeling it a few inches to and fro, 'easy to push outside - should you suddenly pop your spats.'

Scott wasn't paying too much attention to the Minister's dry wit, he was in a poor emotional and physical state, and was happy to rest anywhere:

'Thanks,' he said, collapsing onto the settee with exhaustion. He rested back his head and closed his eyes, desperately trying to think what he could do to get himself out of his self-inflicted predicament.

The Minister watched Scott with concern, then strolled over to a small drinks cabinet and poured out a large brandy.

'Here, drink this down, it'll help calm you,' said the Minister soothingly.

Scott reached out a hand expecting a drink, only to see that the Minister had his back turned, and was actually talking to himself. The Minister downed the brandy with one gulp:

'Ahhh, that's better,' he said wiping his mouth, whilst Scott watched in bewilderment.

'Now, Mister Flowers...' said the Minister, turning to face him.

Scott froze:

'How the hell did you know who I am?'

'This is small village, Mister Flowers, news travels fast.... especially when a man throws himself out of a pub window....and it's not even a Friday night.'

'I see,' said Scott, accepting the plausible answer.

'I don't know what you've done, but I've also heard that there's a lot of money being offered to the one that finds you,' continued the Minister gravely.

This sent Scott into a state of panic:

'I need sanctuary, Reverend,' he tearfully pleaded.

'I'm sorry Quasimodo, old chap, but 'sanctuary' doesn't always work with the underworld,' said the Minister brashly.

Scott stopped to think, he knew this to be true, and suspected that Donald wouldn't let the small matter of a church stand in the way of getting to him; even if Donald were a devout Christian, he would probably pay a couple of heathens to go in and get him. Scott became increasingly distressed:

'What am I gonna do?' he asked helplessly.

'Rest up, you're safe here for the moment,' the Minister reassured. 'Here, let me get you another drink.'

After a short while, the Minister, who had left the lounge to make a series of phone calls, returned to find Scott asleep on the settee. The Minister smiled to himself as he watched Scott resting peacefully, and tried to wake him by gently shaking his shoulder:

'Mister Flowers.....' he said softly.

Scott was in a deep sleep and didn't move. The Minister was about to shake Scott's shoulder again, when he glanced down and spotted small droplets of blood on his brand new beige carpet. He stared at it numbly for a few seconds, unsure how to react, but

somehow managed to let his Christian nature prevail -
he shrugged his shoulders and smiled:

'Oh well, it's only a carpet,' he said to himself,
seemingly unaffected. He slowly positioned his mouth
directly over Scott's ear, then suddenly screamed like
a lunatic at the top of his voice:

'ARGHHHHHHHH!!!!'

Scott was up like a shot. Nervous and disorientated:

'What happened?! Where am I?!'

'It's okay,' said the Minister calmly, 'you were
having a nightmare.'

Scott was unsure, he couldn't remember anything
about a dream. He checked his surroundings and
slowly calmed as he remembered the reason why he
was at the vicarage. But he was also baffled by the
painful ringing in his ear, and shook his head as he
struggled to hear.

'You have to leave now, my son,' said the Minister.

'Sorry?' said Scott, with finger in his ear trying to
unblock it. 'I didn't quite catch that.'

The Minister raised his voice and resorted to using
sign language - which he did expertly:

'I'M AFRAID IT'S NO LONGER SAFE FOR
YOU TO BE HERE!...' he yelled, slowly and
deliberately, whilst simultaneously signing with his
hands: *You've ruined my carpet, you bastard*. Then
he continued '...I'VE ARRANGED FOR A CAR TO

TAKE YOU TO ANOTHER PARISH!' again simultaneously signing: '*Now you can just fuck off*'.

Scott was still holding his pounding ear, but had managed to hear the Minister on that occasion, and acknowledged by nodding.

'Come!' shouted the Minister, and swiftly led the way - out from the lounge, through a long corridor, through a library, through a small office, along another corridor and then back into the lounge. Scott had struggled the whole distance limping in absolute agony, desperately trying to keep up, and was bemused to find himself back where he started. It was a satisfying journey for the Minister, he took a great deal of pleasure in seeing Scott in excruciating pain – a small vengeance for his carpet. The Minister didn't give Scott any time to ponder on the pointless tour of the vicarage:

'Come!' he shouted, and led him straight back out into the corridor.

This time, after a very short walk, they reached a side entrance. The Minister opened the door ajar, just wide enough to see a silver Ford Mondeo waiting close by with the engine running. He opened it slightly wider, checking that there was no one in sight. When he was satisfied, he grabbed Scott by the shoulder and quietly pulled him towards the doorway.

'READY!!!' bellowed the Minister into Scott's

'good' ear, causing Scott to flinch.

'Arghh. Yes,' said Scott, in considerable discomfort.

'Then run, my son!!' ordered the Minister. And with that, aggressively shoved Scott out of the door - but, at the same time, deliberately slipped out a foot, tripping Scott and sending him sprawling headfirst onto the footpath.

'Run!! As quick as you can!!' shouted the Minister.

'Yes. Thank you, Reverend,....' said Scott in a daze, as he staggered to his feet, '...for all your help.' And continued limping towards the car.

'God be with you, Mister Flowers,' said the Minister calmly. Then with a swift flick of the wrist, he slammed the vicarage door shut with an almighty *BANG!* causing Scott to jump.

A rear door of the Mondeo was open, and Scott clambered onto the back seat, closing the door behind him. Scott noticed that the driver was another Minister – a frail man in his 50's with thinning silver hair, silver rimmed glasses, and wearing a dog collar. He turned to face Scott:

'Please cover yourself with the blanket and keep well down, my son,' urged the driver.

He had warmth in his voice, and a kind looking face, which Scott found comforting. Scott nodded, he grabbed the blanket on the seat next to him and lay flat out of sight, completely covering himself as the car pulled away.

3:29PM

Professor Pringle was still on his quest for capital, and found himself sitting in the interview room of the 'Southwest' high street Bank, blushing with embarrassment. On a table close by was a computer monitor with smoke streaming from the rear.

'I am so sorry,' said Pringle. 'I really don't know how that happened.'

The bank manager, Richard Denver, a balding, middle-aged and rather frumpy head of the branch, was seated opposite Pringle, looking perplexed.

'No,...' said Denver, with an element of sarcasm, 'the tea just seemed to *jump* out of your hand.'

'Yes, most extraordinary,' agreed Pringle with fascination. Then, using mime, attempted to re-enact the moment the teacup leapt from his hand – which he repeated several times over, while Denver silently watched in bewilderment.

Pringle suddenly jumped to his feet:

'I don't mind having a quick look at it for you,' he said, manically rummaging through his coat pockets.

'NO! Please!' insisted Denver in a panic. 'The insurance will take care of that.'

'Are you sure?' asked Pringle, still searching through his coat. 'I have a screwdriver...' he explained, producing a tin of cat food from his pocket.

'Positive!' replied Denver abruptly, wondering what kind of lunatic he was confronted with. 'Please sit!'

'Oh, okay,' said Pringle, feeling affronted.

As Pringle sat, his elbow caught a ceramic table lamp, sending it crashing to the floor – *SMASH!*

Denver remembered his stress reducing techniques and began counting to ten. Pringle cowardly avoided looking down at the damage – the sound alone told him it was a write-off:

'Will the insurance take care of that as well?' he asked tentatively.

Denver had reached ten but was still agitated. He picked up Pringle's loan application form and aggressively brushed off some spots of tea:

'This business loan you're after, Mr Pringle...'

'Probably seems a little unusual,' said Pringle with a nervous smile.

'Unusual?...That's one way of describing it,' said Denver, wondering if he should call the authorities to have Pringle certified – but decided that he would be happy just to see Pringle off the premises without further damage to his office. He elected to take the direct approach:

'I'm sorry, but without collateral, I can't help you.'

'But...aren't you the bank that likes to say 'Yes'?' asked Pringle in confusion.

'NO!...' snapped Denver bluntly. 'We're definitely the bank that enjoys saying 'No'!'

'Oh,' said Pringle, taken aback.

'Now please don't touch anything on your way out,' pleaded Denver, clutching onto as many loose items as he possibly could, in preparation for Pringle's departure.

4:12PM

The silver Mondeo carrying Scott drove into the construction site for the new 90,000 seat Wembley Stadium. The structure was midway through completion, and the partial erection of the sports stadium was already an awesome sight and clearly visible for miles around. The construction team were working flat out, with cranes, tractors and trucks constantly on the move.

The Mondeo cruised into the tunnel entrance that will ultimately be reserved for team coaches, and pulled up near the players' entrance close to the pitch. The driver shut the engine off and turned to the back seat where Scott lay hidden under a blanket:

'You can come out now, Mr Flowers, we're here,' he said reassuringly.

Scott emerged from under the blanket:

'Thank Heavens,' he said, forcing a smile and straining his eyes to readjust to the light.

A few seconds passed as his blurred vision came into focus, then he froze - first in disbelief, then with fear. Standing at the front of the car wearing an evil grin was Donald Kelly, his sidekick Mickey just behind him. It was the last thing Scott had expected to see. He looked at the driver, who smiled slyly; the face that Scott thought was warm and endearing at the start of the journey now appeared sinister - Scott looked back at Donald – the two were clearly in cahoots, that much was obvious, but their relationship was the least of his worries. Scott was panic stricken – he needed to act fast to have any chance of escape, but he didn't have any time to react. The rear doors were thrown open and The Twins leant in and dragged him out. The driver smirked as he watched Scott being bundled away. He ripped the dog collar off from around his neck and tossed it nonchalantly onto the driver's seat.

4:20PM

Dealer pulled the Range Rover up on a quiet road not far from his home in Buntleyford village. He looked across to Bolt in the passenger seat, who was still sulking from being kept in the dark, and smiled to himself. Pulling the keys from the ignition, he turned to the rear seat where Bat sat alongside Sally - still heartbroken and in her bridal dress.

'Right,' said Dealer enthusiastically, 'Bat, you go sort out the nosh.'

'Right,' replied Bat with zeal, and was off.

'Bolt, you go see 'ow me horses 'ave done,' continued Dealer.

Bolt paused for a moment, he was extremely suspicious about the bet, and fed up with Dealer, but chose not to question him on this occasion. He reluctantly exited the car in a huff.

'Sally, you're comin' with me,' said Dealer to his sister, who just sat numb with despair, staring aimlessly out of the window, not listening to anything being said.

Dealer climbed from the car and assisted Sally out - she could barely stand, yet alone walk. He put a loving arm around her waist to prop her up, and gently kicked the door shut. They had begun a slow stroll towards Dealer's home, and hadn't got more than a few steps, when Betty Samuels spotted them from across the road:

'Oh Danny!' she called out.

'Oh bollocks,' said Dealer to himself, recognising her distinctive voice.

Betty ran over, and was startled by Sally's appearance.

'Oh my. Are you alright, my dear?' asked Betty with genuine concern.

'No,.....' said Sally with tears in her eyes. 'I've been shafted.'

'Oooo. Nasty,' said Betty sympathetically.

'On my wedding day,' continued Sally.

'Oh you poor thing,' said Betty, feeling Sally's torment.

'By my own brother!' shouted Sally, then burst into hysterical crying.

'Oh Danny, how could you?' asked Betty, clearly disturbed.

'It's not like that,' said Dealer brushing it aside as a trivial matter, '...she's fine.'

Betty was astounded by Dealer's callousness:

'Yes...I can see that,' she said sarcastically.

Dealer quickly grew impatient:

'Look, was there somethin' you wanted, Betty?'

'Well, I was going to ask about some fundraising, but now is probably not a good time,' she replied, more concerned for Sally's wellbeing.

'Actually,' said Dealer, having second thoughts, 'now is a very good time.'

Betty was bemused. 'It is?' she wondered, glancing over to Sally and prompting Dealer to take at look at his distraught sister - wailing uncontrollably.

'Absolutely,' replied Dealer, who was suddenly all smiles. ''ow much ya need?'

Betty was knocked off-balance by the question:

'Well….' she said, racking her brain for an answer, but distracted by Sally's suffering. '...about £14,000,' she eventually replied, dubious as to where the question was leading.

Dealer lifted Sally's hand to reveal her sparkling diamond engagement ring, he scrutinised it for a brief moment:

'Hmmmm...' he said, mentally estimating its value.

Betty watched in disbelief as Dealer quickly and forcibly removed the ring from Sally's finger.

Sally suddenly realised what was happening:

'No!!!' she screamed.

Dealer tightened his hold around Sally's waist while she desperately tried in vain to reach the ring in his other outstretched hand.

'There ya go Betty, that should cover it,' said Dealer, casually slapping the ring into Betty's hand.

Sally was an emotional wreck:

'My ring, my engagement ring!!'

She feebly tried to escape the clutches of her brother, but had little energy. Dealer winked at Betty then dragged Sally away:

'Come on you,' he said, in a manner normally reserved for a pet dog.

Sally was practically walking backwards as Dealer carted her away:

'My ring, my ring, my ring,' she cried, pleading with Betty with an outstretched arm.

'Yeah, yeah, yeah,' said Dealer uncaringly. 'It's goin' to a good cause.'

'I hate you Danny!' screamed Sally. 'I hate you! You're not my brother, YOU'RE THE DEVIL'S ARSE-HOLE!!'

Betty stood with the ring in her open-palmed hand, dumfounded:

'Nice family,' she mumbled to herself.

At that moment Fanny Tattle appeared from nowhere and stood alongside Betty - she had witnessed the entire drama.

'Oh yeah,' she calmly said to Betty, 'never buy a house next to Lucifer's anus.'

4:33PM

Buntleyford village hall had been beautifully laid out for Sally and Quinton's wedding reception. Mildred Watts' five-tier wedding cake adorned the main table – it was a magnificent sight, standing 4 feet in height, with intricate icing patterns, and topped with figurines of the bride and groom, looking uncannily like Sally and Quinton.

A dozen waiters in smart red velvet jackets, white shirts and black bow ties were on standby, all clearly bored and restless - they had been waiting for several hours for the wedding guests to arrive.

The French headwaiter, who had been pacing the hall and pulling his hair out for the past two hours, was relieved to see Bat as he strolled in. He dashed over to him and, in a very broad French accent, asked:

'Ahh Monsieur, where ees Monsieur Dempsey and the wedding party?'

'It's off,' replied Bat.

'Off?' queried the headwaiter, visibly shocked.

'Off!' repeated Bat. 'Cancellated-a-mondo,' he

continued, believing the headwaiter was having a hard time understanding English.

'But what about all the food and the staff? What shall we do?'

Bat produced a wad of cash from his pocket, and broke into a slow pidgin English - in an accent that bizarrely seemed to cover most of Europe:

'Senor Dealer 'e say you take'a dis spondooly and do us a nicey yum yum din din take-away for familesy of cinco,' he explained, holding up four fingers. 'Then ye can buggary offey home. Comprende?'

Bat stuffed the wad of cash into the headwaiter's top pocket while the headwaiter looked on in bewilderment, not understanding a single word he had just heard.

'Do...you...speak...English?' asked the headwaiter hesitantly.

'Cheeky fucker,' replied Bat, clearly offended.

He reached out and aggressively pulled the headwaiter towards him:

'Listen, frog breath,' said Bat, losing the cartoon accent and switching back to his normal voice, 'stop fuckin' about and do me a doggy bag, or you'll be goin' home to the tadpoles with a French loaf up yer arse.'

The headwaiter understood Bat's instruction clearly enough that time, and nervously nodded in agreement.

'Good man,' said Bat patronisingly.

At that moment, the immense white tower of the wedding cake caught Bat's eye. He released the headwaiter and strolled over to it - to double-check. He was right, it was the wedding cake, he could smell the fresh vanilla cream:

'Yummy, yummy, yummy,' said Bat, rubbing his hands together and licking his lips with excitement. 'Guess they won't be needin' this then.'

He swiped the groom figurine from the top of the cake and tried to take a bite - *CRACK!* - it was made of porcelain and rock solid. Bat squirmed as it nearly broke his teeth, and he instantly plonked it back on top of the cake.

'You bastard!' he exclaimed to the headwaiter. 'You haven't fuckin' cooked it yet!'

Moments later Bat had left the village hall with a carrier bag brimming with cartons of food. He happily whistled 'The Wedding March' as he walked along a quiet village road, heading back towards Dealer's home.

Bat was hungry, and the food was on his mind. Without paying any due care or attention, he veered out into the road just as a Luton box-van approached at speed. The driver was Edmund Woodstock, a burly man in his mid 40's with a mass of tattoos on his arms and shoulders. He had a reputation for being brutally hard and uncompromising, and enjoyed a good scrap - which he frequently had, especially after a good night's boozing. Edmund blasted his horn and slammed on the brakes, swerving across both sides of the road, screeching to a halt a few yards from Bat - who didn't break stride or flinch, and was still merrily whistling.

In the back of the van there was chaos, as eight illegal immigrant building site workers from Kosovo were thrown violently by the sudden stop and had ended up in a heap on the floor. The workers were poor and shabby, and barely spoke any English - but found themselves in the UK working for peanuts as part of an illegal ring fronted by the unscrupulous Woodstock. What Bat didn't know when he stepped out in front of the van, was that Woodstock and his workers were on their way to a local construction site for which Councillor Plummer had taken a large back-hander to ensure planning permission would be granted. Plummer was also pocketing 50% of the workers' pay by using Woodstock's 'workforce' in the construction.

The van's windows were open, and Woodstock leant out – absolutely irate:

'Why don't you look where you're fuckin' goin', twat?!!!!' he yelled.

Without showing any change of emotion, Bat veered back towards the driver and, as he approached, unleashed a right hook – *WHACK!* – landing on the button with Woodstock's chin.

'That's *'Bat'*, you tosser,' said Bat, feigning outrage that Woodstock had got his name wrong.

Woodstock slumped onto the steering wheel - out cold.

Bat calmly continued his journey, swinging the food bag and merrily whistling 'The Wedding March', unperturbed by the incident. As he passed the Colonel's front garden, the Colonel, in his army jacket and medals, sprang up from behind the hedge. He watched Bat walking away, then looked over to the van to see Woodstock sprawled over the steering wheel.

'Hmmmm,' said the Colonel with suspicion, and continued his hedge trimming as though nothing had happened.

The illegal immigrant workers had managed to pick themselves up and were relatively unscathed. They were dazed by the incident, but also concerned by the silence outside the van. While they looked at each other with uncertainty, Kosovon worker, Destan - one of the few that could speak a little English - took it upon himself to try and find out what had happened. He knocked gently on the front of the box:

'Mr Woodstock. Sir. Are we there yet?' he asked tentatively, in a broad Kosovon accent.

Woodstock was still out cold. The gentle knocking got louder.

'Hello, Mr Woodstock!' shouted Destan. 'Edmund! EDMUND!'

5:25PM

Maureen Coe was lying on her side huddled up in a ball on her bed, with the house phone lying on the pillow next to her. It was usual for her husband Jerry to call her four or five times in a day, but not only hadn't she heard anything since his departure that morning, despite the many messages she had left on his mobile, but she'd also received a number of phone calls from Donald Kelly's sidekick Mickey – plus a personal visit from Mickey and The Twins wanting to know where he was. They were polite enough, and she had even invited them in; the worry and stress on Maureen's face alone conveyed that she genuinely hadn't a clue as to Jerry's whereabouts, and they had left shortly afterwards on a promise that she'd call if she heard anything. But this was not normal, and Maureen had a sickening feeling deep in her gut that something terrible had happened. She kept thinking about Jerry's last words to her - about receiving some kind of 'bonus' - words that kept echoing in her head, and she was beating herself up for not probing him about it.

She caressed her protruding stomach - her unborn child - and her eyes began to fill:

'Please, please, please,' she pleaded with the phone, willing it to ring, desperate to hear her husband's voice.

She suddenly sat up alert - she thought she heard something move in the kitchen:

'Jerry?' she wondered.

She was quickly up, and went to check. The apartment was silent and so small that it didn't take long for her to realise that she was alone. She thought how ridiculous she was being; she would have heard the front door open had Jerry come home - she figured it had been her mind playing tricks, or probably just wishful thinking. The short moment of hope passed, and the overwhelming feeling of gloom quickly returned.

She was about to turn back to the bedroom, when she stopped - there was an envelope on the kitchen table with her name:

'MAUREEN'

hand-written on it. She was convinced it hadn't been there earlier: She had cleared the kitchen table twice that day already, how could she not notice it? It wasn't Jerry's handwriting, that much she knew for sure, but then she remembered Mickey and The Twins, and thought that one of them must have left it when she had invited them in, but she couldn't remember any of them going into the kitchen - it was all very baffling.

She picked up the envelope and tore it open - a keyring fell out into her hand; it had a single door key attached, along with a thin black security fob. She looked at the keyring with curiosity, then removed the letter that accompanied it and began to read.

The first paragraph knocked her for six, her heart sank into her stomach and tears streamed down her cheeks. She collapsed backwards onto a kitchen chair, devastated. She held the letter in her trembling hands and bravely forced herself to continue reading.

After the initial shock and horror, there followed a feeling of uncertainty and disbelief, followed by an element of relief and hope, quickly followed by anxiety and fear - by the time she had finished reading the letter, it felt like she had been dragged through just about every human emotion possible, and she didn't know what to think or believe anymore. The only thing that felt real was the keyring that she clutched in her hand.

6:15PM

The Wembley Stadium construction workforce had turned in for the day, and the site was serene but for the low rumble of a nearby truck.

Scott, having taken a considerable beating at the hands of Donald, was bound and gagged, and held upright by The Twins. His face had been badly battered and bloodied, one of his eyes practically closed from the swelling around it, but Donald had ensured that Scott was still conscious.

'Well, Flowers. What can I fuckin' say? This is your lucky day, old son,' said Donald with sarcasm.

Tears rolled down Scott's cheeks – he was terrified to the core and fearing the worst. He had 100 grand of Donald's money at his apartment that Donald wasn't remotely aware of – and that would be serious bargaining power had his mouth not been firmly out of commission, but the gag was so tight that he couldn't even squeal. There was nothing he could do, but pray, as The Twins dragged him to the edge of a large pit – the size of a human grave.

'You always did love football,' continued Donald, 'well, now you're about to become part of footballin' history!'

Donald beckoned to his boys, and The Twins obliged by throwing Scott face down into the pit. Scott hit the ground hard, and then struggled as he tried to flip himself onto his back. He could hear a truck rev its engine, the roar drawing closer. It had taken all of Scott's remaining strength to turn himself over, but having succeeded, he wished he hadn't, as his worst fears were staring him in the face. Panic set in, as a cement mixer backed up to the edge of the pit, and cement began to pour on top of him.

Donald watched with sadistic excitement, adrenaline pumping at the sight of Scott helplessly squirming, soon unable to move little more than his head as the cement gushed out. Mickey was standing alongside The Twins manically laughing out loud; it was just like watching his favourite comedy show on TV. The Twins were statuesque - watching with arms folded and legs astride, cold, seemingly unaffected by Scott's terrified face as it began to submerge.

They say in situations like this your whole life flashes before you, but for some strange reason, Scott reflected on the single magpie that landed on his windowsill that morning which he hadn't saluted – in that moment he was convinced the 'bad luck' theory was more than a myth. Scott struggled for air, he stretched out his neck, lifting his head as high as it would go, but it was hopeless, the cement very quickly engulfed him and kept gushing until the pit had filled to the brim. Donald signalled to the driver and the mixer's engine was turned off.

There was an eerie moment of silence as Donald and his gang stood by the pit watching for any movement. A final air bubble came to the surface followed by complete stillness as Scott was laid to rest in the foundations of the new Stadium. Donald was satisfied and turned to walk away, breaking into the famous football chant:

'You're not singing anymore, you're not singing anymore...'

6:23PM

At the vicarage, the Minister was in his lounge sitting with his feet up, in front of a huge plasma TV screen. He was holding a bulky envelope, which he tore asunder to reveal a wad of cash. He didn't bother counting it, he just ecstatically threw the bundle into the air, showering himself with the falling £20 bank notes.

'YES!!!' he yelled jubilantly, then laughed. There wasn't an ounce of remorse for his ill-gotten gains or for turning Scott in - he had finally cracked.

He picked up a giant marijuana-filled spliff from an ashtray and took in a long draw, quickly chased down by a huge mouthful of his favourite brandy.

On the TV there was a porn movie; a man was going at it - doggy style - with a girl on all fours:

'Oh God, yes, yes, Oh God, yes...' she groaned in ecstasy.

The Minister's eyes were opened wide, he was mesmerised and excited:

'Now, that's what I call 'praying'!' he said, with an evil smile.

6:28PM

Professor Pringle was weary and despondent as he opened the front door to his run-down home. Before he could close the door he was greeted by his cat, Eros, who weaved in and out of his legs, with tail high in the air, purring with excitement to see him, and hoping his next meal had just arrived. Pringle picked Eros up:

'Hello Eros,' he said gloomily. 'Another disastrous day, I'm afraid.'

He made his way to the lounge and slumped himself down in his favourite rickety chair, placing Eros on his lap. He stroked his cat affectionately, as he removed the notebook from his pocket and opened it out.

'Looks like I'm slowly running out of options,' he said, looking at the long list of high street banks that had all been crossed off.

'I need money - I need to continue my work,' he explained to Eros with a sense of desperation. 'I'm far too close to quit now.'

He closed the notepad dispiritedly:

'Trouble is, Eros old boy, I don't think anyone's taking me seriously.'

Eros was still purring for food, and Pringle suddenly remembered:

'Oh, I got you this...' he said, producing a tin of cat food from within his coat pocket.

Eros suddenly screeched - then leapt from Pringle's lap and bolted from the room as if he had just been trodden on.

'What on Earth?' said Pringle.

He quickly followed Eros into the kitchen, and was concerned to see his cat trembling, and scratching at the back door, anxious to get out.

'What's got into you?' asked Pringle in confusion. 'It's only cat food,' he explained.

He opened the back door, and Eros raced out.

'How extraordinary,' said Pringle, who had never seen his cat act in such a manner.

He returned to the lounge shrugging off Eros' bizarre behaviour, but stopped dead in his tracks when he noticed a neatly folded sheet of paper in the chair where he had just been sitting. The Professor was completely thrown, as it certainly wasn't something that had fallen out of his pocket, and he was convinced that it wasn't there when he first sat down – or was it? Pringle began questioning himself. He approached with caution, still trying to fathom how it had got there, but eventually picked it up and opened it out - it was a letter addressed to him. He began reading, and the more he read, the faster his heart rate became.

In a sudden fit of paranoia, he spun around in full 360-degree circles, searching in all directions, as though someone might be in the room with him. His heart was pounding like a jackhammer – so hard that it felt like it was about to burst from his chest.

7:00PM

Bolt was pissed off, rattled and on edge as he walked swiftly along the same stretch of road where earlier, Bat had nearly had his comeuppance. As he crossed the road, he slowed down when he spotted two uniformed policemen opening up the back of a Luton van. Curiosity got the better of Bolt, who surreptitiously approached.

Inside the van, the group of illegal immigrant workers were extremely worried. They had given up on Woodstock responding to their cries, and had resigned themselves to the fact that there was no way out, unless they were let out. But their worst fears had been realised when the doors were opened by the local police.

Destan nervously smiled:

'Political asylum?' he asked the two coppers hesitantly.

The policemen looked at each other astounded by their discovery, and were immediately on the radio, calling for assistance.

Bolt had seen enough. He turned to continue his journey and noticed the Colonel in a nearby front garden still trimming his hedge. Bolt could only see the top half of the retired officer who was still dressed in his army jacket and medals. As he approached, the Colonel spoke:

'Strange day we're having,' he said, snipping away.

Bolt was intrigued and stopped:

'Now, why would you say that?'

'Haven't you noticed?' replied the Colonel who stopped trimming and looked up at Bolt with raised eyebrows.

'What?'

'It's the 7th hour.... of the 7th day.... of the 7th month,' explained the Colonel in a very slow and sinister voice.

Bolt was captivated, he wasn't too sure what it all equated to, but it had been one the strangest days he had ever encountered. After a short, dumbstruck moment, Bolt looked at his watch to check the date:

'No it ain't! We're in the middle of fuckin' May!' he exclaimed.

'Are we?' asked the Colonel, clearly puzzled.

'Yes!' snapped Bolt.

The Colonel looked mystified:

'Oh...my mistake,' he said, brushing it aside. 'Still feels bloody odd to me.' And continued trimming his hedge, leaving Bolt more fed up than he was before.

Bolt was about to walk away when he noticed a bright vibrant pink colour gleaming through a small gap in the privet hedge just below the Colonel's waistline. It struck Bolt as being an odd colour to be part of an army uniform, so he leant over the hedge to take a closer look: The Colonel was wearing a sexy pink pair of women's panties, pink suspender belt, black stockings and pink stiletto heeled shoes.

'Yes,' agreed Bolt in bewilderment, 'bloody odd.'

As he slowly backed away in disgust, his attention was directed to the roaring sound of a motorcycle speeding towards him. He span around just in time to see the Minister on his Harley Davidson, doing a 50 mile-an-hour wheelie along the whole stretch of road. The Minister was attired in a pair of torn Levi jeans, a purple bandanna tied around his head in place of a crash helmet. His tasselled black leather Harley biker jacket, which used to bear the slogan 'JESUS LOVES ALL', had been cunningly modified by the Minister to read 'JESUS LOVES ALE'. He was screaming at the top of his voice as he passed:

'WOOOOOOOOOOO!!!!'

Bolt watched with mouth agape:

'Extremely fuckin' odd,' he said.

He turned to continue on his journey but was confronted by Fanny Tattle who dropped to her knees and started beating the pavement with her hand:

'It's a madhouse!!! A MADHOUSE!!!!' she yelled.

Bolt looked at her in astonishment. Then tentatively side-stepped around her:

'Alright?' he said as he passed - not at all interested in a reply.

Fanny looked up at Bolt and smiled:

'Fine,' she said calmly - albeit still on her knees.

Fanny knew most people in the village but didn't recognise Bolt – she saw this as a window of opportunity:

'You're not looking to buy a house in the area, are you?' she asked optimistically.

'Yeah right,' replied Bolt, and was off, heading towards Dealer's home.

'I'll give you a good price!' she shouted after him.

Bolt blanked her and continued his journey. Fanny tried to follow - hobbling on her knees.

'Hey, what the hell, we're all friends here!' she yelled, 'you can have the damn thing for nothing!' - thinking it would draw Bolt back, but she was still ignored.

Fanny gave up and stopped. She watched Bolt heading off into the distance:

'Great investment, Fanny,' she said to herself, 'can't even give the friggin' thing away.'

The Colonel had abandoned his hedge, and

approached Fanny from behind.

'Need a hand?' he asked, reaching out to help her up.

Fanny turned around to see the Colonel in all his glory; half Gaddafi – half Marilyn Monroe, but completely bonkers.

'Take your mitts off me, you damn tranny ape!' she said, shrugging him aside.

The Colonel was affronted, and stood with one hand on his hip, pouting in a rather camp manner as he watched Fanny hobble away on her knees.

7:14PM

Donald was sitting alone in his office anxiously awaiting news. Jerry's disappearance had got him worried; he had never known his bookkeeper to go walkabout before, and this had prompted him to check the ledger against the amount of cash sitting in the office safe – and they didn't tally by a long shot.

There was an opened bottle of Scotch on his desk, and a double shot poured into a cut crystal glass. He checked his watch again, clearly agitated. He knocked back the drink in one gulp and slammed the glass down, then poured out another large shot. At that moment, Mickey and The Twins entered. Donald was up on his feet:

'Any word?'

'Not good, boss,' replied Mickey. 'Jerry's wife said he ain't been home or called her all day. She's worried sick.'

'Fuck,' said Donald with annoyance.

'And then we hear - a body's been washed up on the riverbank,' continued Mickey.

'And?!' asked Donald impatiently.

'I'm pretty sure it's Jerry, boss,' answered Mickey - for once showing some feeling.

Donald was stunned.

'Description to a T, boss,' continued one of The Twins.

'Knife wounds in the chest, boss,' said the other Twin.

Donald felt sick to his stomach, and slowly sat:

'Fuck,' he said. '... And my money? there's a 100 grand missing!'

Mickey and The Twins shrugged their shoulders, they hadn't the foggiest.

There was a brief moment of silence while Donald tried to absorb the news. Mickey and The Twins waited patiently.

'Thanks boys,' said Donald in a daze. 'Look, get back out there and see if you can find out anythin' else.'

'Sure thing Boss,' said Mickey, and beckoned to The Twins to follow.

As the office door closed, Donald looked across to his briefcase that still held the Picasso paintings. It suddenly dawned on him that whatever had happened to Jerry, the first port of call for any police enquiry would be on his doorstep, and there was every chance he would be the prime suspect. The last thing he needed was to be caught with the paintings – time was not on his side.

He picked up his drink and downed it in one, grabbed a set of keys from the desk drawer and securely locked the office door. He returned to his chair with the briefcase, which he placed on the desk and quickly opened up.

Donald was an uncharacteristic bundle of nerves, beads of sweat had appeared on his forehead. He poured himself another large Scotch and knocked it back, trying to calm himself. Then he removed the two rolled up Picasso masterpieces, and sat holding them in his trembling hands. He couldn't afford to be caught with the paintings, and now, with little chance of shifting them, Jerry's original suggestion of what to do with the Picasso's seemed his best option – maybe his only option. But he was torn; he also knew that destroying classic artwork would haunt him for years to come. The two emotions were battling with each other.

'Fuck it,' he said, reluctantly making a bold decision.

He reached for a silver desk lighter, ignited a flame, and slowly brought it towards the paintings. With the flame a few inches away, Donald hesitated, it was the hardest thing he had ever had to do, his hands were shaking uncontrollably.

'Come on, do it, for fuck's sake,' he said, trying to psyche himself up.

He took in a deep breath, and decided to go for it. But as the lighter drew closer and was about to touch, the flame dwindled to nothing and died. He tried several times to re-ignite it, sparks were shooting from the flint, but no flame. Strangely, Donald could see the funny side of this, and even let out a small sigh of relief.

'It must be fate,' he said with a nervous smile.

Suddenly, there was a thunderous knock on the door *BANG! BANG! BANG!*

'OPEN UP! THIS IS THE POLICE!'

Donald's heart sank into his shoes.

7:23PM

Maureen Coe was in London's Waterloo standing across the road from a very posh-looking block of apartments. She was wearing a pair of dark shades, a headscarf and long coat – concealing the fact that she was heavily pregnant. As she stood looking at the building, Maureen was overwhelmed by a feeling of boldness, one she had never felt before; compulsion mixed with fear. She unfolded the letter that she had found in her kitchen and double-checked the address - it was the correct place. She slipped on a pair of white cloth gloves – the pair that she had worn on her wedding day, and produced the 'keyring' that came with the letter. Taking a couple of deep breaths, Maureen made her way across the road towards the main entrance.

As she approached, her heart rate increased tenfold, she wasn't sure where her courage was coming from, but she felt she had nothing to lose – and was desperate to either confirm or dismiss the information in the letter. A CCTV camera outside pointed directly at the main door and Maureen purposely positioned herself to avoid facial contact. She held the key fob over a black pad – and a red light, just above it, instantly turned green. She pushed the door open and entered: The fob had worked – and the reality that the contents of the letter could be genuine hit her. She began to shake, her breathing erratic, legs trembling beneath her. She purposely avoided the elevator, for fear of another surveillance camera, and began to climb the stairs, growing more nervous with each step. It crossed her mind that the tension could bring on the premature birth of her baby, and she took in more deep breaths to try and calm herself.

Maureen soon reached the third floor and walked a short distance to apartment number 17. She lifted her arm to knock – but hesitated; she wondered what she would say should the door be answered – but couldn't think straight. She decided to gamble, and knocked, gently at first, but then harder and with confidence - constantly checking the corridor for any nosy neighbours that might appear. After a short while she knocked again - louder and longer - but still no answer. Taking the key in her trembling hand, she inserted it into the lock and turned it – the door opened. One last look over her shoulder and she entered - quietly closing the door behind her.

The apartment was an eye-opener for Maureen, she had never seen such a luxurious place, she marvelled that some people could live in such wonderful surroundings.

Her heart was pounding relentlessly as she slowly crept her way into the front room. She glanced around briefly, then walked over to the window and peered out; it was a breathtaking view overlooking the river Thames, with St Paul's Cathedral in direct view on one side, and Big Ben, with the Houses of Parliament, to the other:

'So this is how the other half live,' she said to herself.

Maureen didn't dwell on the surroundings for long, she wanted to get out as soon as possible. But as she turned, she noticed a framed photo on the wall, and stopped to look. It was Scott Flowers, dolled up in a tuxedo for a night out, with his arm around someone she didn't recognise - The Dealer. She glared at Scott with resentment, then turned away to explore the rest of the apartment.

She crept along a hallway pushing open each door as she passed, until she swung open the door to a bedroom. She entered, and stood at the doorway absolutely flabbergasted; resting on the bed were four huge piles of cash - exactly where Scott had left them that morning.

So far, everything she had read in the letter was 100% accurate, and after the initial shock, which lasted several minutes, Maureen didn't know whether to laugh or cry, and subsequently did both. What she really wanted to do was collapse with exhaustion, but she managed to hold herself together. Wiping away the tears, she produced a large plastic carrier bag from within her coat and quickly piled the money into it, before making a hasty exit.

7:32PM

Bat and Sally were seated together on a black leather settee in the lounge of Dealer's home. Sally, still in her bridal gown, sat numbly looking through her tear-filled eyes into oblivion, feeling little more than an empty shell. Every so often Bat would look across at her, desperate to start a conversation of any description to break the uncomfortable silence, but he'd hear a heart-wrenching sigh emanating from her direction and quickly turn back, too afraid to open his mouth.

The lounge was vast, and Dealer was seated in the bar area opposite them, smugly puffing on a giant cigar with a glass of brandy in his hand. It was the way he tended to finish off most evening meals, and he had just had one of the best takeaways ever – the catering from his sister's wedding, on which he had spent a small fortune. Despite the sorry state of his sister, for which he was directly responsible, Dealer was feeling self-righteous and content, and was patiently anticipating Bolt's return.

The door opened and Bolt entered, he was not at all happy. He produced a moneybag from within his jacket, and threw it venomously towards Dealer who caught it with one hand.

'Is this what I think it is?' asked Dealer, with a huge smile.

'Why do I get the impression that you're not really surprised?' replied Bolt, extremely peeved.

'What is it?' asked Bat.

'It's his fuckin' winnings,' explained Bolt. 'Every horse came in first.'

'Wow,' said Bat in amazement. ''ow much ya win, Dealer?'

'Ooooo I reckon, about... a hundred and seventeen thousand, four hundred and twenty three pounds, and forty-one pence,' replied Dealer nonchalantly, and opened up the bag to check his winnings.

'Forty-two pence,' corrected Bolt, who was not in the least bit impressed and highly suspicious of Dealer's sudden mathematical skills.

'They must 'ave worked it out wrong,' smirked Dealer.

Sally was astonished, but thought she may have misheard things in her dazed state. She stopped crying to double-check:

'How much did you say?'

'Fuck,' said Bat in wonderment, '120 quid is about

as much as I've ever won.'

'Okay, Dealer, what the hell is goin' on?' demanded Bolt, getting scared, and annoyed with Dealer's secrecy. 'This whole day has been fuckin' ridiculous!'

Just then the house phone began to ring in the hallway – the perfect opportunity for Dealer to avoid any further questions:

'Get that, will ya Bolt,' he said coolly. 'Tell 'em I'm busy.'

Bolt looked daggers at Dealer before reluctantly leaving to answer the phone, slamming the door behind him and causing Bat to flinch. Dealer was unfazed by Bolt's little tantrum, in fact he found it quite amusing. He calmly began counting his winnings - which had been neatly bundled up into £1000 packages.

'What ya gonna do with all that dosh, Dealer?' wondered Bat.

'It's your lucky day, Bat,' replied Dealer, 'there's a grand for ya.'

He threw a bundle towards Bat who didn't see it coming and hit him square on the face – *SMACK!*

'Wow...Cheers, Dealer. What a mate!' exclaimed Bat excitedly.

Dealer put another bundle to one side:

'A grand for Bolt,' he explained. 'And for my dear

sister, there's thirty gees.'

Dealer picked up the huge wad of cash and walked over to Sally. He held the money out to her and smiled:

'Does this make up for fuckin' up your weddin'?' he asked innocently.

Sally looked at the cash blankly, then looked back at her brother and erupted:

'You can't buy me, you bastard!!' she screamed. 'I want my Quinton!!'

She slapped Dealer's hand away from her, and burst into tears. Dealer tentatively placed the cash down on the armrest next to her:

'Well, look, let's just leave it there,' he said, slowly backing away. 'You may change your mind.'

He sat himself back down at the bar just as Bolt returned looking as white as a sheet.

'You alright, Bolt?' asked Dealer.

'It's Stan - your stockbroker,' said Bolt.

Dealer smiled knowingly:

'Good news is it?'

'As if ya didn't know,' replied Bolt sarcastically. 'Bool Technology shares - 73 percent up on the day. He advises you to sell.'

'What does he fuckin' know?' said Dealer dismissively. 'I'll hold 'em a while longer.'

Dealer chucked a £1000 bundle towards Bolt, who

caught it with one hand.

''appy Christmas,' said Dealer with a smile.

Bolt was wound up to the point of wanting to chuck it back at Dealer and tell him where to shove it – but the moment passed quickly, and he managed to bite his lip.

''ere Dan, what are ya gonna do with the rest of the cash?' asked Bat.

'85 grand of it's goin' into a new business venture,' explained Dealer.

'Oh yeah,' said Bolt, ever the cynic, 'what sort of business?'

'All in good time, Bolt,' explained Dealer.

7:37PM

Quinton Verani had somehow managed to find his way to Dealer's home, and was outside in the street – completely drunk. He was still in his white wedding suit - now looking somewhat dishevelled; the top few buttons of his shirt were undone, his tie had been pulled loose and hung to the side, in his hand was a bottle of Vodka - most of it he had already demolished. His hair was a mess, he was distraught, disorientated and, like Sally, an emotional wreck.

Fanny Tattle happened to be passing Dealer's home when she spotted Quinton hovering outside:

'Oh, here we go,' she said, rolling her eyes.

She watched as Quinton swayed and stumbled over his own feet into the nearest tree, which he used to prop himself up.

Fanny was seething; it seemed wherever she turned there was something untoward happening in her neighbourhood, and even though on the scale of things a distraught drunk in the street seemed pretty lame, she was just sick to death with it all. She stood watching Quinton for a short while as he tried several times to leave the support of the tree, then approached apprehensively and, for no explicable reason, felt compelled to engage in conversation:

'Let me guess,' she said, gaining Quinton's attention, 'you must be the other half of the happy couple,' she observed with a deadpan expression.

Quinton looked at Fanny and his eyes began to fill.

'Oh please don't,' said Fanny, now wishing she'd crossed the road.

Quinton tried to speak: 'Er...uhm.' - was all he could mutter before bursting into tears.

'Oh great,' said Fanny to herself, 'now you've made the groom leak.'

Feeling partially responsible for stirring up Quinton's already fragile emotions, Fanny half-heartedly tried to calm him:

'Ahhhh,' she said, patting him gently on the shoulder, 'Boo Boo lost his nookie?' she asked, in the patronising way that one might comfort a two-year-old that had lost a toy.

Quinton nodded, still unable to talk or turn off the waterworks.

'Never mind,' she continued in the same manner, 'I'm sure she'll pop up somewhere.'

Fanny turned Quinton to face Dealer's home, then put her mouth close to his ear:

'Have you tried looking in the enchanted castle?' she whispered, waving her hand across it - as though it were a mystical wonderland.

'No...' winced Quinton, snivelling and wiping his nose with the back of his hand. 'Not yet.'

'Well, what are you waiting for?' asked Fanny, 'an invitation from the fiery Godfather?'

Quinton's eyes were fixed on Dealer's home, he hitched his trousers and took a swig from the bottle. Fanny sensed he was gaining courage.

'Go get her, Tiger,' she whispered. And with that, gave Quinton a gentle push in the right direction.

Quinton staggered onto Dealer's property:

'Sally...Sally...' he wailed.

Fanny puffed out her cheeks with relief, pleased to be rid of him:

'Well, good luck,' she blurted, whilst walking backwards and waving - leaving Quinton to his own devices. 'Watch out for that top window,' she continued, remembering what had happened to Jimmy Todd, 'unless of course you enjoy a good old fashioned house-dangle.'

Quinton hadn't a clue what Fanny was on about, but wasn't remotely interested. He continued staggering towards the house.

Fanny was still walking backwards:

'And if you're ever in the area again,' she shouted,

'please don't hesitate to keep going 'til you're somewhere else!'

By this time Quinton was oblivious to everything Fanny was saying, he was off on a drunken quest to find his fiancée. He strongly suspected her to be inside the house, but even in his drunken stupor he wasn't bold enough, or stupid enough, to attempt a forced entry into a gangster's home – he knew it would be suicide. So he figured he'd do the next best thing, which was to shout his beloved's name as loud as he could, in the hope that she would come out. He took another mouthful of Dutch courage:

'Sally!' he yelled.

Inside the house Sally perked up and was suddenly alert, she thought she'd heard Quinton's voice outside, but she wasn't sure:

'Quinton?' she wondered.

Dealer had also heard the voice and was extremely pissed off that Quinton might be outside:

'Oh no,' he exclaimed.

Quinton's voice got louder:

'Sally, I love you!! Where are you?!!!' he shouted.

This time there was no doubt in Sally's mind:

'Quinton!' she yelled, filled with nervous excitement.

She jumped to her feet and dashed towards the door but Bolt's towering figure was blocking the doorway - and Sally's exit. Sally struggled to get past, desperately trying to find a gap to squeeze through.

'Let me go!' she cried in frustration. 'Quinton!'

But Bolt stood his ground and there was no way out for her. She gave up and dashed towards a window.

'I'm coming, Quinton! I'm coming!!' she cried.

En route, Sally ran headlong into a floor-lamp, with three misted glass shades, sending it crashing to the floor – *SMASH!*

'I'm coming!!' she yelled – but the train of her wedding dress had caught on the corner of a stand-alone book cabinet, which slowed her down. She swung around and yanked at the train, sending the cabinet crashing to the floor and books flying everywhere – *CRASH!*

'I'm coming!!' she screamed again, turning back to continue her journey, and knocking aside a pedestal holding a china figurine of Al Capone – sending it crashing to floor and shattering into pieces – *SMASH!*

'Fuck's sake,' winced Dealer.

'Oh, that reminds me,' said Bat, listening to all the commotion – which sounded to him exactly like the passionate throes of love making, 'that cheap Viagra is fuckin' useless!' he proclaimed.

At last Sally had reached the window and could see Quinton outside in the front garden on his knees, drunk and distraught, tears streaming down his cheeks

– he looked a wreck, but he was still the best thing she had ever seen. She flung open the window:

'QUINTON!!' she cried.

'SALLY!!' cried Quinton.

'HEATHCLIFF!!' bellowed Bat.

'Shut up, Bat!' said Dealer, not at all amused. He turned to Bolt. 'Go get 'er then!' he ordered.

Bolt glared at Dealer - annoyed that Dealer couldn't be bothered to get up off his backside to sort his own sister out, but again chose to keep schtum. He reluctantly made his way over to the window – kicking aside the carnage that Sally had left in his path.

By the time Bolt had reached her, Sally had already managed to get one leg outside, and was desperately trying to haul the other leg through, but her bridal dress was proving to be a hindrance and she was struggling. Quinton was up off his knees, tears streaming, his arms spread open wide:

'Yes, Yes,' he cried, urging Sally to come to him, but too pissed to think to go and help.

Bolt stood watching Sally struggle, he couldn't help but feel sorry for her, and he was so narked with Dealer that part of him wanted her to escape. As he watched, Sally managed to pull most of her train through and was about to launch herself out, when Bolt thought better of it:

'Come on Sally, inside,' he said, putting a secure arm around her.

'No, no, let me go! I want my Quinton!' said Sally, weeping wildly.

Bolt dragged her back inside.

'Wait for me, Quinton!!' she screamed in distress. 'Wait for me!!'

Quinton watched her disappear from view, then, in frustration, swung around booting a nearby bush, sending leaves flying everywhere. He collapsed back onto his knees:

'I will!! I won't move!!!' he cried.

Bat had heard enough:

'I'll get rid of him,' he said with vigour, and was up, marching towards the window like a man on a mission - focused and determined. When he arrived at the window, Quinton was only a few yards away, but Bat was looking straight through him. For a split second, Quinton quaked in his shoes, but then had to check over his shoulder, as he couldn't seem to figure out where Bat's multidirectional eyes were looking. Bat's face contorted as he tried to focus:

'There's no one there, Dealer,' he said, dumbfounded.

Dealer tutted. 'Just shut the window, and get back in 'ere!'

Bat took another long and hard look outside,

shrugged his shoulders and closed the window.

Bolt was still holding onto Sally - who by this time looked a horrifying state. She had cried so much that the black mascara had run from her eyes down her cheeks and neck, and onto her beautiful white bridal gown - she was beginning to resemble the bride of Frankenstein.

'Why do you hate him so much, Danny?! Why?!! What has he done?!!' she hysterically demanded to know.

'Nothin'.....yet!' said Dealer. 'But he will! Trust me.'

Bolt was vexed - not only with Dealer's outrageous behaviour throughout the course of the day, but also with the lack of respect he had been showing his sister, and he thought she deserved an answer:

'What do ya mean '*nothin' yet*'?!' yelled Bolt. 'Are you fuckin' psychic, or somethin'?!'

'What's the time?!' asked Dealer, completely blanking Bolt's question.

'I tell ya what, Dealer, why don't you use some of that money, and buy yourself a fuckin' watch!' replied Bolt who had had enough, and started to mock Dealer. '*"What's the time? What's the time?"*'

'Well, what's the time!?' demanded Dealer.

'I got it!' said Bat jumping in. He looked at his watch and his eyes crossed as he tried to read it. 'It's er... Ooo it's about...Ooo,'

'Oh don't,' said Dealer, exasperated.

'Sorry Dan...' said Bat in defeat, pulling his sleeve down over his watch and hoping that no one had noticed. 'I must 'ave left it at home.'

'It's quarter to, alright?!' snapped Bolt.

At last an answer. 'Thank you!' exclaimed Dealer, getting up and heading towards Sally:

'Now go an' get the door,' he ordered Bolt, and took hold of his sister.

'What?!' said a bemused Bolt.

'The door,' repeated Dealer.

'What fuckin' door?!' shouted Bolt.

Dealer held a finger up and summoned silence. A few seconds passed while they waited, then to everyone's astonishment the doorbell rang - *DING DONG* - Dealer smiled and smugly put the cigar in his mouth.

'You are one weird fuck today,' said Bolt, glaring suspiciously at Dealer.

Dealer took a tight grip of his sister, and turned to Bolt:

'Just get the door and show 'em in,' he said coolly.

Bolt left in a huff, while Dealer threw Sally down onto the couch next to Bat:

'Now you just sit there and don't fuckin' move, alright?!'

'Yes, your Royal Anus!' replied his defiant sister.

Bat was astounded by the insult, but also highly amused and laughed inwardly – he knew there weren't too many people that would get away with a cutting remark like that.

Bolt returned looking miffed. He was closely followed by an odd looking man in his 60's, dressed in an old green tweed suit and bow tie. He had a small pair of silver rimmed glasses perched on the end of his nose. Bolt moved aside to allow him to enter. The man was carrying an old tatty leather briefcase, which he clutched tightly to his chest, the contents clearly valuable to him. He appeared jittery and hyper, and scanned the room several times in a squirrel-like manner, with his head jerking in all directions, before eventually approaching Dealer:

'Are you the one they call 'The Dealer'?' he asked tentatively.

'That's me,' acknowledged Dealer proudly.

The stranger was so relieved at finding the right person, that without thinking, he pushed his briefcase into Bolt's chest so he could properly greet Dealer:

'Pringle, Professor Pringle,' he said, excitedly shaking Dealer's hand.

'Pleased to meet ya,' said Dealer.

Pringle was all smiles, until he glanced to his side and realised that Bolt was holding his precious briefcase. Pringle had to do a double take, he had no idea as to how it had got there. He quickly released Dealer's hand and snatched his briefcase back, clutching it tightly to his chest again, eyeing Bolt up and down in a very disapproving manner, whilst Bolt looked on in bewilderment. Dealer found Pringle's erratic behaviour amusing and smiled to himself as he led the way to the bar. Pringle closely followed.

'Did you know there's a man outside crying his heart out?' asked Pringle.

'Yeah I did,' replied Dealer uncaringly. 'Can I get you a drink?'

Sally burst into another bout of tears, burying her head into Bat's shoulder. Bat froze, uncertain of how to react, he pondered for a second, then patted Sally on the head like a pet puppy. Pringle looked over to Sally, puzzled by her wedding attire.

'That's my sister, Sally,' explained Dealer. 'She nearly got married today.'

'Oh,' said Pringle with excitement. 'How..... romantic,' he continued meaninglessly. He then turned to Dealer and lowered his voice. 'Er...could I have a word with you in private, Mister Dealer?'

'Oh no,' replied Dealer, calmly laying down the rules, 'whatever's gotta be said, has gotta be said in front of all of us.'

'It does?' asked Pringle.

'It does,' confirmed Dealer.

'Oh...okay,' said Pringle somewhat surprised, but happy to go along. 'Well, I'm coming to you as a last resort.'

'Yeah?' said Dealer.

'Yes,' said Pringle apologetically. 'I'm afraid that everyone else thinks I'm... completely mad, and won't have anything to do with me.'

Pringle had got Bolt and Bat's full attention, while Dealer just smiled and poured himself a large brandy.

'Go on,' said Dealer, prompting the Professor to continue.

'Yes, er, you see, I've discovered a way ...in theory ...to er....well ...... time travel,' revealed Pringle.

Sally suddenly stopped crying and slowly looked over to Pringle, intrigued. Bolt was thrown by the revelation, he glanced over to Dealer with suspicion - Dealer coolly swallowed a mouthful of brandy, he was looking smug and in no way surprised.

Pringle gave them a moment to digest the information, and frantically looked at each of them in turn, trying to gauge their reaction.

Bat was confused: 'What, like a villa in Spain?' he asked.

'Shut up, Bat,' snapped Bolt. He turned to the Professor. 'What do you mean 'Time Travel' ?'

'I know it sounds insane,' explained Pringle with a

sense of excitement, 'but I have found a way to send things back in time. Not people... yet...but certainly small inanimate objects.'

Dealer removed the 'letter' from inside his jacket pocket:

'Like a letter?' he enquired, holding it up for all to see.

Both Bolt and Sally were staggered. Pringle knew nothing about the 'letter' but believed it to be plausible:

'Yes,' he agreed, '...like a letter or such.'

Bolt was stunned:

'Letter? Fuck.' he exclaimed, as the reality hit.

'Look, cut a long story short - I need financing,' said Pringle with desperation. 'I can't carry out my work without capital.'

'Let me take a wild guess,' said Bolt sarcastically as he recalled the new 'business venture' that Dealer had been extremely cagey about, '...you need 85 grand.'

'Yes,' said Pringle exuberantly. 'But...how did you know that?' he continued in astonishment.

Pringle quickly opened his briefcase and pulled out all his facts and figures:

'... I have a full breakdown here,' he explained.

As Pringle held the papers out for Dealer to see, his elbow hit a china vase, sending it crashing to the floor - *SMASH!* - Pringle flinched with embarrassment as it shattered into pieces, but the vase was ignored - all eyes slowly turned to Dealer, holding the 'letter'.

Dealer wasn't interested in seeing Pringle's papers – he was confident that they were all in order, he sat back and puffed on his cigar contentedly.

'A letter...from the future?' wondered Sally in awe.

Dealer raised his eyebrows and smiled, his gesture confirming her assumption.

'May I?' asked Sally calmly, holding out an expectant hand.

Dealer didn't hesitate, he handed the 'letter' to her, which she opened out and began to read with interest.

The Professor was baffled by the 'letter' and his mind was working overtime trying to fathom what was going on. He could see that Dealer and Bolt were focused on Sally as she read, so he didn't interrupt.

Sally was mesmerised by the contents of the 'letter', her heart pounding faster with every word, scaring her as much as it did Dealer when he first read it. By the time she had finished reading, she was gobsmacked. She took a moment to reflect on all the day's events, then looked over to the £30 gees that Dealer had left resting on the arm of the settee. She was in a zombie-like state as she slowly rose to her feet, dropping the 'letter' into Bat's lap. Bat picked up the letter and tried to read it, while Sally steadily headed towards the lounge door. She paused at the doorway and looked back at her brother:

'Dan, I'll be back in a minute,' she said calmly, making her way into the hall.

Bat was struggling with the 'letter', he rotated it several times, then moved his glasses up away from his eyes – that didn't work either. He tried it at arm's length, short range - up close to his nose, and even tried squinting – he turned to Dealer:

'It's in Scottish!' he exclaimed with frustration.

Bolt tutted: 'Fuck's sake, give me that,' he said, snatching the letter from Bat's hand.

Moments later, Sally swung open the front door and could see Quinton in the garden – still on his knees and swigging from a bottle of Vodka. As she gathered up the train of her wedding dress into her hands, Quinton lifted his head - his face instantly brightened. He abandoned the bottle and was up on his feet with arms outstretched:

'Sally! My love, my darling,' he called out to her, tears of joy streaming down his cheeks. '....Come to me!!'

Sally smiled affectionately and strode towards him, she seemed ready to run into his arms for the perfect Hollywood ending, but as she approached, she suddenly launched a foot – aiming straight between Quinton's legs...

Quinton was shopping in a very upmarket jewellers. Janet, the attractive sales assistant, was wrapping Sally's engagement ring. She couldn't seem to take her eyes off Quinton, and was obviously attracted to him.

'Well, if she turns you down, you can always give me a call,' said Janet, half-jokingly.

Quinton was pleasantly surprised, and began to flirt:

'Really?' he asked with a suggestive smile.

'Sure,' replied Janet, returning the smile. 'I know a good thing when I see it.'

Quinton licked his lips and produced a business card from his breast pocket:

'Tell you what,' he said, holding out the card, 'why don't you give me a call this weekend?'

Janet was happy to take the card:

'I might just do that,' she replied, with every intention that she would.

At that moment, the store manager walked into earshot. Janet quickly hid the card and flipped back into work mode. She handed a small bag over to Quinton:

'Excellent choice, Mr Verani,' she said, politely smiling. 'I'm sure she will be over the moon.'

Quinton read the situation and quickly followed her lead. He politely smiled back:

'Thank you.....fingers crossed,' he said, acting apprehensively.

Janet held up her crossed fingers.

A short while later, Quinton was at the public park, striding across the grass on his way to meet Sally. He had just passed an attractive woman, Caroline Carter, who had deliberately slowed down to gape at his good looks - she couldn't take her eyes from him.

As Quinton passed, she about-turned and slowly walked backwards ogling Quinton's toned physique heading away from her. She let out a heavy lustful sigh:

'Phwooar.'

As Caroline turned back around to continue her journey - SMACK! – she walked headfirst into a tree and collapsed in a heap on the ground. Quinton had taken a brief glance back over his shoulder and had seen Caroline's mishap. She was attractive enough for him to feign concern and rush to her assistance.

Caroline was dazed and had a nasty graze on her forehead. Quinton knelt down next to her and gently lifted her onto his lap. He cradled her in his arms, stroking the hair away from her face.

'Are you okay?' he asked.

As Caroline's blurred vision began to focus, she saw a sunlit angelic aura around him.

'Have I died and gone to heaven?' she asked.

Quinton laughed. 'Women normally only say that after I've made love to them,' he replied.

Caroline smiled. 'Is that so?' she asked coyly.

'Oh yes,' said Quinton, in a playful manner.

'Well,... maybe I can find that out for myself.'

'Who knows?' said Quinton. 'Maybe you will.'

Caroline was floating on cloud nine as she snuggled into Quinton's arms.

Sally's foot was on direct course, and connected really hard between Quinton's legs – *CRUNCH!* – Quinton let out a high-pitched squeal, then held his testicles in excruciating pain. His eyes slowly crossed, as he keeled over in agony. Sally gathered her train, about turned and marched back into the house.

DEALER

I DARE SAY THAT THIS LETTER HAS COMPLETELY
FREAKED YOU OUT. I HOPE YOU'VE CALMED
DOWN, NOW THAT YOU'VE HAD A CHANCE TO
RANSACK YOUR HOUSE LOOKING FOR AN
INTRUDER.

RECOGNISE THE WRITING? YOU SHOULD DO,
IT'S YOURS. THAT'S RIGHT YOURS. IT'S
DEALER HERE, WRITING TO YOU FROM THE
FUTURE. I KNOW YOU ARE NOT GOING TO
BELIEVE ME, SO HERE'S WHAT YOU NEED TO
DO.

FIRSTLY, DON'T WASTE ANY TIME, GO SEE
OUR OLD MATE JOHN STANTON. HE OWES YOU
A FAVOUR, ASK HIM TO CHECK THE HAND-
WRITING.

NEXT, YOU NEED TO GET YOURSELF DOWN TO
HARRINGTON BOATYARD AND KEEP YOUR EYES ON
A WHITE BOAT, THE 'OWMUTCH'. AT AROUND
11.30AM SCOTT FLOWERS WILL MURDER A
MAN THEN DUMP HIS BODY IN THE RIVER.
WHY? BECAUSE SCOTT OWES HIM MONEY -
BIG TIME. RATHER THAN SETTLE HIS DEBT HE
WILL CHOOSE TO ELIMINATE HIS LENDER. YES
SCOTT FLOWERS, THE VERY MAN YOU HAVE
TAKEN UNDER YOUR WING ALL THESE YEARS, IS
NOTHING BUT LOW LIFE SCUM - AND YOU NEED
TO SEE THIS FOR YOURSELF, THAT BASTARD WILL
TRY AND PIN THIS ON YOU.

AFTER THAT, YOU'LL HAVE NO DOUBT THAT
THIS LETTER IS FOR REAL, AND THIS CAN TURN
OUT TO BE THE GREATEST DAY OF YOUR LIFE
AND MINE, AS IT WILL HAVE A KNOCK ON
AFFECT FOR ME IN YOUR FUTURE.

HERE'S WHAT YOU DO — BUY SHARES (AS
MUCH AS YOU CAN) IN BOOL TECHNOLOGY
PLC — THESE WILL SOON GO UP OVER 900%.

LISTED BELOW YOU WILL FIND THE WINNERS
AT CHEPSTOW RACE MEETING TODAY.   A $20
EACH WAY ACCUMULATOR WILL NET YOU A
COOL $117,423.41.

SCOTT WILL INTRODUCE YOU TO DONALD KELLY
REGARDING SHIFTING SOME STOLEN PAINTINGS.
STAY CLEAR OF HIM.   DONALD WILL BE
ARRESTED WITHIN A WEEK, AND THE BASTARD
WILL FINGER EVERYONE WHO WAS INVOLVED.

TWO WORDS TO GET COUNCILLOR NEIL PLUMMER
PERMANENTLY OFF YOUR BACK AND ON THE PAYROLL —
EDMUND WOODSTOCK.

TONIGHT AT PRECISELY 7.45PM YOU WILL
HAVE A VISIT FROM A PROFESSOR PRINGLE. BE
NICE TO HIM, HE'S THE GEEZER THAT WILL
INVENT THE TIME TRAVEL MACHINE. PRINGLE
WILL NEED 8S GEES TO GET IT UP AND
RUNNING.   YOUR HORSE WINNINGS WILL
TAKE CARE OF THAT.

OH AND DON'T LET SALLY MARRY QUINTON.
HE WILL BEAT HER BLACK AND BLUE, AND FUCK
OTHER WOMEN BEFORE THEIR HONEY MOON IS
EVEN OVER. - I MAY GO DOWN FOR WHAT I
DONE TO THAT SHIT.

I'LL WRITE AGAIN AS SOON AS I CAN.

THE DEALER

THE WINNERS AT CHEPSTOW RACE MEETING
TODAY.

Time	Horse	Time	Horse
2.45	DAYBREAK	3.25	SIDE GLANCE
4.05	DIM DANCER	4.45	PRINCE HERON
5.20	RAZZET	6.00	DISTANT CLOUD
6.40	KEY HOLE		

About The Author

Tony Royden is a London-based composer/song writer/music producer who has successfully managed to establish himself in many diverse fields within the music industry; from composing stage musicals to producing top 20 pop/dance records and musically directing a prime time BBC TV chat show. Tony can boast over 80 BBCTV title music commissions - including The BAFTA TV Awards, 3 National Lottery shows (including The National Lottery Wright Ticket), EMMAs 2002, Hot Wax, Song For Europe, Grandstand, The Other Half, The O-Zone, The Booker Prize, Winter Olympics, Radio 1 Road Show, Michael Palin presents The Grierson Awards, Mind Games, Equinox and The Red Nose Awards - to name but a few.

In 1987, Tony had great success with his musical 'Tanya', for which he wrote music, words, and screenplay. The story of a girl's struggle to beat her addiction to drugs, 'Tanya', was sold to and produced by the BBC - and has been shown in its entirety throughout Europe. The Dealer is Tony's first novel, and promises more for the future.